TWEED FICTION BU

Also by Christian Burch

The Manny Files

Hit the Road, MANNY

Christian Burch

Atheneum Books for Young Readers
New York ✣ London ✣ Toronto ✣ Sydney

Atheneum Books for Young Readers ✢ An imprint of Simon & Schuster Children's Publishing Division ✢ 1230 Avenue of the Americas ✢ New York, New York 10020 ✢ This book is a work of fiction. Any references to historical events, real people, or real locales are used fictitiously. Other names, characters, places, and incidents are products of the author's imagination, and any resemblance to actual events or locales or persons, living or dead, is entirely coincidental. ✢ Copyright © 2008 by Christian Burch ✢ All rights reserved, including the right of reproduction in whole or in part in any form. ✢ Book design by Kristin Smith and Jessica Sonkin ✢ The text for this book is set in Egyptian 505 BT Roman. ✢ Manufactured in the United States of America ✢ First Edition ✢ 10 9 8 7 6 5 4 3 2 1 ✳ Library of Congress Cataloging-in-Publication Data ✳ Burch, Christian. ✳ Hit the road, Manny / Christian Burch. — 1st ed. ✢ p. cm. — (The Manny files ; #2) ✢ Summary: As the Dalinger family travels across America in a rented recreational vehicle, Keats grows more accepting of the attention-getting behavior of their "manny"—male nanny—especially after a visit with the manny's parents on their Wyoming ranch. ✳ ISBN-13: 978-1-4169-2812-6 ✢ ISBN-10: 1-4169-2812-X ✢ [1. Family life—Fiction. 2. Automobile travel—Fiction. 3. Self-acceptance—Fiction. 4. Nannies—Fiction. 5. Sex role—Fiction. 6. Brothers and sisters—Fiction. 7. Homosexuality—Fiction. 8. Humorous stories.] I. Title. ✢ PZ7.B91583Hit 2009 ✢ [Fic]—dc22 ✢ 2007040260

**To my Sugar Bear,
who is his own kind of brave**

Remember me? My name is Keats. I was this
year's spelling bee champion for our elementary school. I was the first fourth grader to ever
win. Usually fifth graders win because they
have had an extra year of spelling practice and
are more mature and calm under pressure. My
win made the front page of the newspaper.
There was a picture of me holding my trophy,
with my smiling classmates surrounding and
congratulating me with pats on my shoulder. It
was a posed photograph, kind of like the pictures of the movie stars in the Hollywood issue
of *Vanity Fair*, except nobody had their shirt
unbuttoned or puffy lip injections. The photog-
rapher stood on top of a desk, so the picture
looks like it was taken from the sky. His pants
were unzipped. We were all giggling in the
picture because Craig said, "X-Y-Z-P-D-Q." My
uncle Max says it all the time. It means "Examine
your zipper pretty darn quick." Dad always

says, "Your cows are getting out," when my zipper is down.

Somebody made bunny ears behind my head in the newspaper photo, but I didn't care. Uncle Max says, "Any publicity is good publicity!" He has a newspaper clipping on his refrigerator with his name in the police blotter from the time he got a speeding ticket on Main Street. "Forty-five in a thirty-five." I don't know what that means, but Uncle Max says it with a bragging smile like it's a big achievement.

Now that I've won the spelling bee, the teachers at school wave to me and say hello like I'm a celebrity. My best friend, Sarah, says that she's surprised that I haven't been asked to be a host of the Miss America pageant. I think she was kidding. Sarah is my best friend and she teases me. She says it's to "keep me down with the real people." She's worried that my winning the spelling bee will go to my head and I will be full of myself like my big sister Lulu.

Lulu is in the eighth grade and is good at everything. Dad says that she's "high strung" because she is always worried about rules and homework deadlines. She's the eighth-grade class president, and instead of trying to get a snack machine in the cafeteria or a new tree planted in the quad, she attends school board meetings and tries to convince the superintendent to "make the curriculum more challenging." Those are her words, not mine. Teachers used to call me Lulu's little brother, but that changed after I won the spelling bee. Now they just call me Keats. I wish they'd call me Champ.

My other older sister is India. She's the exact opposite of Lulu. Dad calls India "mellow" because she never worries about grades or rules. She only worries about hemlines and stitching because she wants to be a clothing designer when she grows up. India is in the fifth grade and is always giving fashion advice to the teachers. Mrs. House, my fourth-grade teacher, used to wear white blouses and long skirts, but she cut her hair and started wearing tight black clothes after India told her that the "peasant look" was over. India didn't say it in a mean way. She never says anything in a mean way. Mom calls her "tactful." Tactful means you can tell the truth without hurting people's feelings. Like when I pointed out Dad's bald spots by telling him they were cute. It didn't hurt his feelings, but it let him know that he had bald spots.

My little sister, Belly, isn't very tactful. She once pointed to a large man at the grocery store who had a long beard and said loud enough for him to hear, "MOM, HAGRID!" Hagrid is the giant, hairy guy in the Harry Potter movies. Mom pushed the cart down the aisle so fast that Belly, who was riding in the seat, dropped DecapiTina, her headless doll, on the white tile floor. Poor DecapiTina. DecapiTina wasn't always headless. She used to be a really pretty doll. Now she's just a dirty old doll body, but Belly refuses to throw her away. She says that she'd still love Mom and Dad if they didn't have heads. I guess she has a point.

Dad laughed when Mom told him the Hagrid story, even though she was trying to get his sympathy and probably a hug. Dad works in an office and wears suits. His job starts each day with two cups of coffee. Mom only drinks one cup each morning, and then she brushes her teeth and eats an Altoid. She says that she has to have fresh breath because she's always talking to people at the art museum where she works. She hangs the paintings and photographs on the walls, and then she takes me to see them to get my opinion. She says I'm good with lines and space and that I will probably grow up to be an architect and that she wants me to build her a modern house. But I want to be a concierge so I can tell people where to eat and what movies to see. T.G.I. Friday's and anything with Johnny Depp in it.

The manny says I would be a great concierge. He's always letting me do things for him like call in for his telephone messages and shine his shoes. The manny is our male nanny. We had a lot of nannies before him, but they were all women. Sarah thinks that if a male nanny is called a manny, then a woman nanny should be called a wanny. Sarah has an odd sense of humor. This spring she told our teacher, Mrs. House, that she was going to give up cigarettes and booze for lent, but not coffee. Mrs. House laughed but looked like Sarah's joke made her uncomfortable, like she might call Sarah's mother and ask to meet with her.

The manny is so much fun. Even Lulu thinks so. She didn't use to. She even tried to get him fired by keeping a list of things that he did that she thought were inappropriate. Like "hickey checks" when he picked her up from school dances. Lulu called her list "The Manny Files." We had a family court about it to decide if the manny should stay. I stuck up for the manny and convinced Mom and Dad that Lulu was power hungry and that she was the only one who didn't like the manny. Lulu likes him now. She figured out that he gives good advice about romance.

"Always have a boyfriend around holidays so that you get gifts."

"Always look your very best, even if you're just running out to get the mail, because you never know where you're going to find true love."

"Never sneeze on a date."

That last one is especially for India, because when she sneezes, she accidentally passes gas. It sounds like this: "Hachooo"-*phhht*, like her whole body is exploding. Then she gets really red faced. Uncle Max calls it a "snoot" because it's both a sneeze and a toot.

My uncle Max thinks the manny's fun too. Uncle Max is my mom's brother. He's a painter, and he likes art just as much as my mom does. Mom and Uncle Max inherited their artistic ability from my grandma. She used to live with us and liked to look at art books with me. Grandma died last summer, but some of her ashes are still blowing around in our yard. We scattered them in the garden that we planted for her. I found some of the ashes next to a lilac bush and put them in between the pages of her favorite Andrew Wyeth art book, which I keep in my top drawer with my underwear. Grandma would get a kick out of being put in my underwear drawer. Grandma got a kick out of a lot of things.

Uncle Max and the manny are roommates, and they're always laughing and hugging. Lulu gets mad at them because she thinks that PDAs are disgusting. "PDA" means "public display of affection." The manny and Uncle Max love teasing Lulu. The madder Lulu gets, the more PDAs they do.

The spelling bee was at the beginning of the school year. Now—*woo-hoo!*—it's the last week of school and, more importantly, the week before my birthday. Mom and Dad say they have a big surprise for me for my birthday. On India's birthday they told her they had a big surprise for her, too. It was her very own sewing machine. She screamed and jumped up and down like a contestant on *The Price Is Right* when she opened it. When I was sick and stayed home from school, the manny and I watched *The Price Is Right*. Now when the manny calls me for dinner, he yells, "Keats Dalinger, come on down!" and I run into the kitchen screaming and guessing how much the Mrs. Butterworth's syrup costs ($3.25).

India used the sewing machine to make us all scarves for Christmas. They were pretty, but they weren't very warm because they were only made out of old T-shirts. Lulu only wore her scarf once because she was afraid the material might have come from the yellow armpit part of one of Dad's old T-shirts. Dad sweats a lot. Mom wears her scarf all the time. Sometimes she wears it wrapped around her head with her sunglasses on like she's Jackie O. Jackie O. was married to President John F. Kennedy, but she wasn't called Jackie O. then. She was the First Lady and is famous for wearing hats made out of pillboxes. It sounds strange to me, but I once saw a girl with a dress made out of credit cards in a magazine, so I guess anything is possible in fashion. After President Kennedy was assassinated, Jackie married a guy whose last name was Onassis; that's why they call her Jackie O. If people called me by my Jackie O. name, it would be Keats D. because my last name is Dalinger, but that sounds too much like a rapper.

I hope my birthday surprise is a lock on my door. Every day when I come home from school, I discover Belly has stolen things from my room. Crayons. Books. Cuff links. I once came home and she had taken all of my *GQ* magazines that Uncle Max had given me after he was done reading them. Belly tore the mouths out of the cover models so that she could stick her lips through the holes and make the pictures talk. She made them say things like, "Oooh, sexy. Kiss her on the lips," and then she wagged her tongue around. Mom saw her do it and decided it would be better if Belly only watched television in the mornings from now on.

Belly talks more than she used to since she turned four. A lot more. And she's really loud. The manny says Belly has a foghorn voice. When she wakes up in the morning, she doesn't get herself out of bed. She likes for Mom to come get her. Belly yells, "MAAAAAAWM! HER NEEDS YOUR HELP!" at the top of her lungs. She also refers to herself as "her" instead of "I" or "me." It drives Lulu nuts. She's always trying to correct her because she says that grammar is the key to getting ahead. I don't know what she thinks Belly needs to get ahead in. She pretty much runs our house.

Belly is so loud that she sounds like that guy on television who builds houses for underprivileged families or families with disabled kids. Except *he* has a megaphone. Mom watches that show on Sunday nights while Dad cooks dinner. Sundays are his day to cook. His specialty is grilled cheese sandwiches and tomato soup. He makes the soup out of a can, but he pretends that it's homemade and hides the empty cans deep inside the trash can underneath paper towels. We pretend that we don't know.

Mom watches the home makeover show and cries. Once there were kids on the show whose bones were really fragile. They called them the "glass children." It was scary because the yeller guy jumped over the "glass children" when he was playing around with them in their new, safe padded room. Mom screamed out loud when he did it and said that he should be given a sedative before he broke one of the children. Lulu says that Belly will probably jump around and scream like that when she's an adult. Dad says that Belly has "Courtney Love tendencies." I don't know who Courtney Love is, but Dad usually says it when Belly's walking around with her dress lifted up or throwing a tantrum on the living-room floor.

The manny watches the show too and points out when Lulu's crying. He doesn't do it so that she knows he's doing it. He taps me on the leg and then points to Lulu when she's wiping her tears away. She started watching the show with a blanket around her head so that we couldn't see her face. But we can still hear her sniffling. Lulu doesn't like people to see her be emotional. She says that she doesn't want the attention. I don't believe her. She also pretends to be embarrassed when the manny teases her, but I can tell she likes it by the way she sings, "Don't . . . stop!" It sounds more like, "Don't stop."

Lulu treats the manny like he's her personal assistant and stylist. She asks him to do things for her like she's a celebrity. Make her hair appointments, get her a bottle of water, pick the green M&M's out of her movie snack.

One time when we went to the grocery store, Lulu even asked him to carry an umbrella over her head because she had seen someone carrying one over P. Diddy in a magazine. Except I don't think his name is P. Diddy anymore. He changes it all the time, like he's running from the law. Puff Daddy. Puffy. Pidizzle.

The manny thought that Lulu had gone too far with her umbrella request. Instead of carrying the umbrella over Lulu, he took it and began singing and dancing. "I'm singing in the rain, and Lulu is ashamed. What a glorious feeling. Lulu Dalinger's her name." He sang it really loudly, so that people were laughing and pointing.

Lulu screeched, "Don't say my name!" and ran into the store to get away from him. When she reached the automatic doors where the shopping baskets were, she tripped on a mop and skidded across the wet floor on her stomach like the penguins from the movie where they walk back and forth to the ocean. I laughed so hard that I nearly wet my pants. Lulu laughed too. Especially when the manny started twirling the umbrella and singing, "Under my umbrella. Ella. Ella. Ella."

Lulu's fun when she doesn't take herself so seriously, or at least that's what Mom says.

3 Lucky Penny

The manny woke me up the next morning by peeking his head into my bedroom door and singing, "Schoolboy! Time to wake up and go to school and learn something so you can grow up and be somebody!" Every time he wakes me up for school, he sings it, and then he throws his head back and laughs. He sings it to Lulu and India, too, except he calls them "schoolgirls." Lulu hates it. She's not a morning person. She's not really an afternoon or an evening person either.

There were balloons all over my room. Not just five or six, but thirty or forty all over the floor. We were celebrating my birthday early because Dad had to go out of town on my real birthday. I didn't care. I hate waiting for my presents. I had to kick through the balloons just to find my underwear that I had laid out for school. I wear striped boxer shorts now, ever since Craig stole my Scooby Doo briefs on our class trip to the swimming pool and wore them like a hat in front of everybody. Craig is a boy who has been in my class for the last two years and used to pick on me. Now we're sort of friends. I don't think he has very many. After Craig wore my underwear like a hat, the kids at school called me Scooby Doo-Doo-Pants for about a month, until my friend Scotty sneezed and a yo-yo of snot came out of his nostril and swung around until he sucked it back in. The kids started calling him Snotty Yo-Yo and forgot all about calling me Scooby Doo-Doo-Pants. They're not very original when it comes to making up nicknames. I would have called him Walking-the-Snot Scott because it looked like he was doing the walk-the-dog yo-yo trick.

Uncle Max and the manny had put the balloons in my room to surprise me. I could tell it was them because I could still smell Uncle Max's Acqua di Parma lotion. He buys it at Saks Fifth Avenue. I have a bottle too. It's one of Uncle Max's old empty ones, but it still smells good.

Uncle Max and the manny stayed for breakfast. When I walked into the kitchen, the manny started to sing, "Hey, Keats. It's your birthday. We gonna party like it's your birthday. We gonna drink chocolate milk like it's your birthday. And you know, we're not gonna cuss 'cause it's your birthday."

The real song has bad words in it and is by a guy named 50 Cent, but everybody calls him Fiddy. India says that his arms are freakishly big, like a bulldog's. I've seen him interviewed on television, and he seems nice. He's been shot nine times and he's still alive. I think he should change his name from 50 Cent to Lucky Penny.

In the middle of the breakfast table was a pile of presents for me. A red box with a white ribbon. A blue-and-white striped one. A gift bag with a picture of Garfield on it. I could tell which one was from Belly because it was wrapped in toilet paper and stuck together with chewed-up gum instead of Scotch tape. She shook it in front of my face until I was so annoyed that I grabbed it from her and opened it. Inside was Lulu's pink iPod. Lulu quickly grabbed it from me and scrolled through the songs to make sure that Belly hadn't erased any of her Simon and Garfunkel.

"Whew! 'Bridge over Troubled Water' is still on here," Lulu said, relieved, looking up to the sky as if God had been watching over and protecting her iPod.

"YOU WANTED A POD," said Belly in her foghorn voice. She was sitting on Dad's lap, and he had to turn his head away from her to protect his hearing.

"Open mine next," said India, grabbing a present from the center of the table.

India's present was wrapped in newspaper. She had painted bright red flowers with yellow middles on it with acrylic paint. Dad admired the paper. He even put on his glasses to see it better. They're bifocals because he's reached that age. He's also reached the age where he has to take Metamucil in the morning to help him poop. I'm not supposed to tell people that any-more. One time I introduced him to Sarah's mom by saying, "This is my dad. He takes Metamucil to help him poop." Then I turned to my dad and said, "This is Sarah's mom. She gets menstrual cramps." Sarah had told me about her mom's cramps. The manny always says to introduce people with a little fact that they have in com-mon, and stomach issues was all I could think of that they had in common.

Inside India's flower-wrapped present was a T-shirt that she had sewn my name across in red velvet letters. I put it on over my collared shirt and put my collar up. India says the preppy look works for me. I always feel like a J.Crew model when I wear my collar up. Like I should be sailing on Martha's Vineyard or playing lacrosse at Princeton.

I opened Lulu's present next. It was wrapped in cutout pictures from old *People* and *Us* magazines. Lulu likes to cut out pictures of celebrities. She and her friend Margo cut out pictures of boys that they think are cute and tape them all over a wall in her bedroom. Lulu calls it the Hot Guy Wall. There's a picture of a tennis player without his shirt on. There's a picture of the boys from *High School Musical*. There's even a picture of a CNN news correspondent. He's a little older than the rest of the "hot guys," and his hair is completely white. Lulu says she likes him because of his "intellect." When Lulu's not in her room, the manny always adds pictures of himself to her Hot Guy Wall. She usually notices after a few days and takes them down and puts them on another wall in her room. She calls that wall her Freaks and Geeks Wall. There aren't pictures of anybody else on the Freaks and Geeks Wall. Just the manny.

I ripped open Lulu's homemade wrapping paper, and Belly grabbed it and cuddled with a picture of a kitten. Inside, the present was a framed picture of Lulu riding a horse. I thanked her but immediately thought I would replace the picture of Lulu with a picture of my friends Sarah and Scotty and me in the frame. The one where we posed for the manny in front of a

SLOW CHILDREN sign and pretended to be running really slowly.

Uncle Max handed me a small box wrapped in squiggly silver wrapping paper. There was a card with it that had a picture of a red-haired boy with a mouthful of french fries. I opened the card and read, *"Keats, we thought you could use this to tune out. Love, Uncle Max and the manny."*

I ripped it open as fast as I could because I already had an idea of what it might be. And it *was*! A metallic blue iPod of my very own. I jumped up and down and hugged Uncle Max and the manny. I screeched, "Thank you, thank you, thank you, thank you, thank you—"

Until Uncle Max interrupted me. "That's what uncles are supposed to do . . . spoil you and make your parents look bad."

The manny said, "I've already programmed it with a lot of songs that I know you like and some that I like so I can borrow it." Then he smiled.

I scanned the playlist: Green Day. The Muppets. Elton John.

The manny loves Elton John. Mom had a kara-oke party for Dad's last birthday, and the manny wore a white suit, with his hairy chest showing, and big white-framed glasses. He sang, "'Oh, Lawdy Mama, those Friday nights, when Suzie wore her dresses tight, and the Crocodile Rocking was out of sight.'" Then he sang in a really high voice, "Laaaaaaa. La-La-La-La-La." I thought the champagne glasses from Mom's toast to Dad were going to shatter. But they didn't. Well, *one* did, but that's because Belly was trying to carry it on her head like the little girl who's fetching water at the end of *The Jungle Book*.

After my iPod frenzy died down, I remembered that Mom and Dad had a surprise for me. I scanned the table, but there weren't any more presents left, just empty boxes and ripped-up wrapping paper. I thought that maybe my present was too big to fit on the kitchen table.

Maybe it was a brand-new car and it was parked in the driveway with a big red bow wrapped around it like people do when their kids graduate from high school or college. I'm too young to drive, but a giant red bow would be really fun.

I was still daydreaming about the giant red bow when Dad asked, "Are you ready for your birthday surprise from us, Keats?" He had his arm around Mom like they were going to spring something very exciting and overwhelming on me. I hoped Mom wasn't pregnant. This was how they stood when they told me Belly was coming. Maybe they would announce that we'd won the lottery and they were going to let me pick out a new house for us. I'd pick something in Nantucket. I like the accent they have in Massachusetts. It sounds wicked cool.

Mom and Dad didn't announce that we had won the lottery. Instead, Mom did a pretend drum-roll while Dad announced that we were going to rent an RV and go on a road trip across America this summer.

"Surprise!" Mom yelled as she raised her arms up in the air and shook her hands. "You've always wanted to take a road trip!"

I had told Mom and Dad that I wanted to go on a road trip on our last vacation, when we were on an airplane and I sat next to a baby who cried the whole time and then threw up milk on my favorite black pants. The baby's mother didn't even notice. She also didn't notice when I stuck my tongue out at her baby. *My* mother noticed and pinched my leg.

Being stuck in an RV with everybody is way different than a lock for my door. I pretended to be really excited so I wouldn't hurt Mom and Dad's feelings. I did a dance that the manny taught me called the cabbage patch, where you march in place and move your arms around in circles in front of you like you're churning butter. The manny did the cabbage patch too. India did the worm. Mom said the manny was coming for moral support. I couldn't tell if he was going to be moral support for her or for me.

I excitedly hugged everyone and ran with India and Lulu to catch the bus. It was the last day of school, and the bus driver was going to let us chew gum.

Mrs. House decided not to give us any more schoolwork since this was the last week of school. She said she was "burned out" on grading papers and giving tests. I can tell that she's burned out. Last week she wore two different shoes, one blue and one black. They didn't even have the same size heel, so she walked lopsided all day, like a pirate. When she asked Craig to stand up and hand out our graded science worksheets, he answered by saying, "Aye, aye, Captain."

I don't think Mrs. House understood Craig's joke because she said, "Oh! I like being called Captain," and wobbled back to her desk.

Instead of schoolwork Mrs. House let us play heads-up seven-up and watch educational videos. We watched a documentary about kids in New York City learning how to ballroom dance. They were really good, but I was disappointed that there weren't more cartwheels and splits in their choreography. Cartwheels and splits would have added some flair. Flair is when you have a talent for something or you make something fancy. I learned the word "flair" last January when Mrs. House said I had a "flair for the dramatic" when she handed back my math quiz. It was really hard, but I only missed one. Before I realized that it was out loud, I shouted, "Hallelujah!" and threw my arms up in the air. I said it so loud that it scared Sarah, and she accidentally knocked over her pencil organizer that she keeps on her desk.

Lulu's class watched educational videos this week too. The manny had to pick her up early from school yesterday because they showed a movie about where babies come from. Lulu said that it made her feel faint and short of breath. Lulu has a flair for the dramatic too. It runs in our family, like freckled shoulders. Lulu was white as a sheet and refused to eat the lasagna that Mom had made for dinner. She kept saying she was having "flashbacks." I thought a flashback was a football player, but India told me that a flashback is when something from your past comes back to haunt you. Like Mexican food does to Dad.

No schoolwork is the best birthday present Mrs. House could have given me. She isn't the only one who's burned out. Last week I fell asleep during a school assembly when the high school band came to our school to play. I woke up and the gym was almost empty and the brass section was emptying their spit valves and putting away their horns. I had to run across the gym to catch up with my class.

The manny is going to bring my birthday snacks this afternoon (caramel apples). But first a guy named Newly is bringing animals that he owns into our classroom to teach us about them. A big snake. Lizards. A baby crocodile. Newly is famous at our school. Most of the students have been to an assembly or a birthday party where Newly was the main attraction. There was even a rumor that he lived with his animals in the basement of the school. There's a big lock on the basement door, but everybody claims to know someone who has seen Newly going in there at night after all the kids have gone home. Craig told me that for after-school detention one time he had to clean out the cages in the basement. I think Craig sometimes makes up stories to get attention. Once he wore a red bandanna around his head for a week and told me that Willie Nelson was his grandpa. Willie Nelson is a singer that has long braids and sings songs about baby cowboys and mamas.

Mrs. House sat down in a chair in front of the class and told us that before Newly came, we needed to come up with questions to ask him.

She handed out little pieces of paper to each of us and had us write a question on it. When we were done, she collected them and read them out loud to decide which ones should be asked.

"'Why is your name Newly?'

"'Is Newly short for Newlton?'

"'Is Newly your first name or last name?'"

Mrs. House rolled her eyes and glanced at the next question. She said, "Oh, here's Sarah's question. I bet it will be a little bit different." And she read, "'Is it true you live in the basement of our school?'"

Mrs. House looked frustrated and asked us if we had questions about the animals and not about Newly. The room went silent, and we looked around at one another and shrugged. She gave up. She knew that we had all grown up seeing Newly's shows and that, by now, it was Newly we were excited to see, not the six-foot python.

When Newly knocked on the door, we all cheered. His cheeks were bright red, like a sunburn, and his white teeth smiled through his thick beard and mustache. Newly brought cages full of reptiles, a few birds, and even a skunk that had had its stink removed. When Newly was telling us about the skunk, Craig passed gas and said really loudly, "Whew! I just had my stink removed too!" We all laughed, even Newly, but Mrs. House made Craig go out into the hallway anyway. We could see his face through the skinny glass window on the door. He kept pressing his lips against it and crossing his eyes. Mrs. House didn't notice. She stayed in the back of the room, away from the snake cages, during Newly's whole presentation. She even clipped and filed her fingernails, which I pointed out to Sarah and said was rude. Sarah reminded me about falling asleep during the band performance last week and told me not to throw stones from my glass house. That's one of Sarah's mom's sayings, "You shouldn't throw stones when you live in a glass house." It means that you shouldn't judge people, because none of us are perfect. When I grow up, I really do want to live in a glass house. I love the smell of Windex.

Newly finished his presentation with an albino cobra. Albino means it doesn't have any pigment or color. Newly kept the colorless snake in its glass cage, but it gave me the shivers, and I stood in the back of the room behind everybody else. We never got to ask Newly our questions. I guess he will stay a mystery for a little longer.

As Newly was packing up his animals and leaving the room, the manny showed up with the caramel apples for my birthday party.

The manny saw the albino cobra and said, "I

love Whitesnake." Then he made hand gestures like people make at rock concerts, except he was making the sign for "I love you" in sign language. He started to sing, "'An' here I go again on my own. Goin' down the only road I've ever known.'" He told me that Whitesnake was a heavy metal band from the eighties who used to have music videos with girls rolling around on the hoods of cars.

"What kind of cars?" I asked.

He didn't know.

Mrs. House knew what he was talking about. She said that she had gone to a Whitesnake concert in Tulsa when she was in high school. She said she still had the T-shirt.

"I'll give you a dollar if you wear it to the next parent-teacher conferences," said the manny. Mrs. House laughed and covered her mouth with her hand. I think she was trying to seem delicate and ladylike, but it didn't work because she snorted and spit on the desk when she laughed.

I can't imagine Mrs. House at a rock concert. She won't even let us walk down the hallway without being in a single-file line. The chaos of a mosh pit would probably "harsh on her mellow." India always says, "Stop harshing on my mellow," when she wants me to stop jumping on her bed when she's trying to paint her toenails.

The manny started telling Mrs. House about our road trip, while I passed out the caramel apples. The kids sang "Happy Birthday" to me. They really screamed it, but Mrs. House was too tired from the school year to stop them. You can get away with anything on the last day of school. Craig still hadn't come back from being sent out into the hallway, but Mrs. House didn't seem to care. His head wasn't in the window anymore. Sarah said that he was probably torturing squirrels on the playground or that he had stolen Principal Allen's Oldsmobile and was fleeing to Texas. I reminded Sarah about throwing stones from her glass house.

Mrs. House had a string of caramel hanging from her chin when she said, "Keats, be sure to stop by my classroom next year to tell me all about your trip." I had to ask her to say it again because I was staring at the caramel on her chin and not listening.

I finally answered, "Oh, I will. It will be so educational."

A comment like that could raise my final grades and maybe even convince her to nominate me for an award like Student of the Year or Best Dressed or Most Valuable Player.

Mrs. House hugged me good-bye. The manny stood there until he got a hug too.

5 Mannytopia!

A week after school let out for summer vacation Dad brought home an RV that had the words CRUISE AMERICA on the side and had a picture of snow-covered mountains and people on bicycles. He had rented it for my birthday surprise trip. When Dad gave us the tour of the RV, Lulu screamed, "This is my seat!" and sat in a booth that was by a table.

The manny whispered to her, "I'm going to steal it when you get up."

She didn't get up at all during Dad's tour, not even to see the tiny kitchen or the bathroom that had a vanity mirror surrounded by lights. Lulu would like it if there were a chair that sat right in front of the mirror. She likes to practice facial expressions in the mirror. Angry. Thoughtful. Surprised to be getting an award.

The RV had one bed in the back (probably for Mom and Dad); one above the driver, which Lulu and India claimed; and the booth folded out into another bed for the manny. The seats were really big, like thrones for kings and queens, and Mom said that they folded down and would make perfect beds for Belly and me. India sat kindergarten style in one and pretended to meditate with her hands on her knees and her fingers pointing toward the roof of the RV.

I sat down in one and said, "This is the most comfortable chair I've ever been in. I could stay here forever."

"Good," said Dad. "Because we'll be driving a long way before we fly back home from Las Vegas."

The manny squealed when Dad said "Las Vegas." He loves Las Vegas.

"Where else can you travel the world in one evening without ever having to change out of your thongs?" he pointed out to India.

"Nobody calls them thongs anymore," said India. "They're called flip-flops. Thongs are different."

"Oh, sorry," the manny apologized as he pretended to adjust his thong underwear through the back of his jeans.

Elton John has a show in Las Vegas at Caesars Palace, and the manny really wants to go. Elton John plays a concert whenever Céline Dion is on vacation or is filming car commercials. She'll be gone when we're in Las Vegas. Lulu tried to find out where she would be by surfing Céline's Web site, but it didn't say. I looked over Lulu's shoulder while she was searching, and I saw that Céline Dion has her own perfume, only it was called a fragrance instead of perfume.

"What do you think it smells like?" I asked the manny.

"Probably like talent and determination, with just the right touch of attitude," he said. "Like Lulu after gym class."

"Your fragrance would be a fruity mix of sarcasm and starched shirts," Lulu said back to the manny in her snotty voice.

"I'd call it Mannytopia, and I'd have candles made too," said the manny, raising his hands in front of him like he was imagining his name in bright lights on a billboard.

The manny started typing on the computer when Lulu was done. He said he wanted to look at the Elton John Web site to see if it would be appropriate to wear a feathered boa to the concert. Elton John's Web site has pictures of him playing the piano and wearing wild glasses with sparkly diamonds around the rims. There's a link on it where you can actually hear a message of his voice. I think it was an old message because at the end he said, "Happy Christmas," and

Christmas was more than five months ago. Elton John has a British accent, like Sarah's mother.

Sarah called to tell me good-bye and asked me to send her postcards from interesting places. I wrote down her address on a piece of paper and put it in my silver money clip. My silver money clip doesn't have any money in it, just phone numbers and old movie tickets. And Sarah's and Scotty's school pictures.

6 Keep on Trucking

The morning that we were scheduled to leave on our road trip, Uncle Max came over. He was going to feed our dog, Housman, and stay at the house while we were away. He couldn't come with us because he was having a showing of his paintings at a gallery at the end of the summer and needed to get some painting done. He said the manny distracts him. The manny distracts me when I'm trying to do my homework by doing handstands.

This is Uncle Max's first official show in a gallery, and he wants the paintings to be perfect. He showed one to me. It was a family around a dinner table. It reminded me of last Thanksgiving, when we had dinner around the dining-room table. When nobody was looking, Belly grabbed Dad's glass of wine and drank it in one big gulp. She thought it was grape juice. There wasn't very much in the glass, but she still talked like a drunk Teletubby for the rest of the afternoon.

She kept saying, "Her loves you, DecapiTina," except it sounded like, "Her lubyu D'captain-a." Mom told us not to tell that story to other people.

Mom had packed an ice chest full of water bottles, juice boxes, grapes, and string cheese. She put it under the table in the RV so we could snack on the road. It's a family trait that we all get cranky when we get hungry. Mom calls it "low-blow sugar." I think it means that you haven't had enough sugar, so you start saying mean things to each other.

We had so much luggage that it wouldn't all fit in the storage closet. We had to pack the rest in the bathroom and jam the door shut. Dad said we needed to not use the bathroom unless it was an emergency, because it would be a pain to unpack all the time.

Lulu sat in the seat she had called a few days before and refused to get up and help pack the RV. She was worried that someone (the manny) would steal her spot. She didn't even get up to go to the bathroom when Dad yelled, "Last call. Use the restroom in the house before we start motoring down the highway. Over."

Dad had started talking in trucker lingo after he had picked up the RV. He kept saying things like "Keep on trucking" and "Over" whenever he was done saying what he was saying.

Uncle Max hugged all of us good-bye. When he hugged me, he said, "Keats, please send me a postcard from all the places that you visit . . . and put interesting facts on them! I yearn to learn!" Then he laughed.

I nodded and remembered the coconut that the manny had sent in my school lunch last year. He had written BE INTERESTING on it in Sharpie, and I kept it on my dresser. I bet we will visit a lot of interesting places, like the world's biggest ball of yarn or a Krispy Kreme, where they make the doughnuts on a conveyor belt.

Uncle Max stood up from me and gave the manny a hug. The manny kissed Uncle Max good-bye. It was really dramatic, like they were on *Days of Our Lives* and they were saying good-bye forever.

"Not in the driveway," screeched Lulu. "That's so inappropriate."

Lulu uses the word "inappropriate" a lot. Usually when Belly jumps on the trampoline without pants on or when the manny tells Belly to pull up her pants because "Crack is whack!"

"Be good," Uncle Max said to the manny. "No teasing the children."

Just then the manny pulled Lulu out of her chair and dropped her on the floor and sat in her "saved" seat.

"Noooo!" Lulu squealed so loudly that Mom looked back from the front seat.

The manny jumped out of the seat and said, "Yessss, Lulu, you have to put your seat belt on, we're getting ready to leave, and it's the law."

Lulu gasped. She doesn't like to be accused of a being a lawbreaker. She called the manny a troglodyte. India told me that a troglodyte is like a caveman. The manny does have hair on his knuckles like a caveman, but I don't think he would ever wear a shirt with only one shoulder strap. In fact, the manny doesn't even wear tank tops. He says that armpits shouldn't be on public display. Lulu thinks it's funny that the manny considers tank tops bad taste but laughs when Uncle Max makes the toot noise with his hand in his armpit.

We waved to Uncle Max as we began pulling out of the driveway. He had Housman in his arms and was making him wave his little paw. Dad honked the horn until we couldn't see Uncle Max or Housman anymore. The manny looked a little sad, like the little boy at the end of *E.T.* when E.T.'s spaceship has come back for him.

"He'll be right here," I said, and pointed at the manny's heart just like they did in the movie. Except my finger didn't light up.

That's when we heard Uncle Max yelling,

"Wait, wait," and saw him running up to the side of the RV. He was holding Belly in his arms. She had gone in to the bathroom, and in our excitement we loaded up and started on our trip without her. And we almost made it.

"I guess you won't be getting the Parents of the Year award this year either," said India, and the manny started to laugh. The manny had said the same thing a few months ago when Belly burped really loudly during one of Mom's friends' wedding ceremony. It wouldn't have been so bad if Belly hadn't thundered in her foghorn voice, "OH MY GOSH! THAT WAS A BIG ONE!" and tried to high-five Dad like they do at home.

After Dad had honked the RV horn, Mrs. Waycott, our neighbor across the street, came out on her front porch. She blocked the sun with her hand, squinted her eyes, and watched Uncle Max hand Belly inside the RV. Mrs. Waycott shook her head as if she was disgusted that anybody could actually forget their child. She was hanging up a new wind catcher. She makes them herself out of the same yarn that afghans are made of. This one was orange and blue. There must be fifty of them on her front porch. They blow in the wind and make her house look like a Mardi Gras parade float. Dad used to call her Crazy Waycott when he thought we weren't listening. "Crazy Waycott's got some hairdo today." "Looks like Crazy Waycott adopted another cat." "Crazy Waycott backed her Buick into her mailbox again." He stopped calling her Crazy Waycott last March when he rode his bicycle by her with Belly in the baby seat and Belly yelled, "PRETTY HOUSE, CRAZY WAYCOTT," and started waving.

As Mom shrugged and smiled at Mrs. Waycott, the manny strapped Belly into her car seat and then kissed Uncle Max again. This one was on the forehead, so Lulu didn't dry-heave.

Dad honked the horn and said, "We're back on track. Over."

"Please don't talk like that anymore," Mom said, flustered. Mrs. Waycott was still on her front porch making judgmental faces. That's what India said.

"That's how we talk in the big rigs, babe," he said to her. I've never heard him call Mom "babe" before. He usually calls her "sweetie" or "hot mama."

Mom stared at Dad without blinking just to let him know how much he was annoying her. Lulu stares at me that way when she wants me to stop singing "Hey Ya!" by OutKast. It's usually when I get to the "Shake it like a Polaroid picture" part and start jerking like a short-circuited robot. Lulu raises her forehead as far as she can and stares at me without blinking. She thinks I stop because I'm scared, but really I stop because it's hard to sing and count the wrinkles in her forehead at the same time. She looks like a shar-pei puppy.

Mrs. Waycott went into her house as we left our driveway, probably to call all of her friends to let them know about the second-rate parents who live across the street. That's what India said. Mom looked worried.

The RV was filled with the excitement of a road trip. Belly was talking nonstop and telling stories about her friend Justin. They weren't really stories because they didn't have a beginning or an ending or a point. They were more like little facts. Like about how Justin eats turkey and cheese sandwiches without the crust. How Justin wears cowboy boots. How Justin wants to marry her when he grows up.

Mom and Dad were in the front seats, and they both had smiles on their faces while they talked about the last time they had gone on a road trip. It was in Dad's little green Mustang that he had in college. They drove to Florida for spring break, but Dad forgot to make hotel reservations and there were no more rooms available anywhere. They ended up staying with Mom's great-aunt Jill at her retirement community. Dad was hoping for a spring break full of girls in bikinis who needed help rubbing on their suntan lotion. Instead, Mom and Dad spent most of their time playing bingo and taking water aerobics classes. Mom says that's where they fell in love.

"It already felt like we had grown old together," Dad added, reaching over and squeezing Mom on the back of the neck. India says it's their secret way of saying "I love you" without having to say it in front of all of us.

India smiled, thinking she was in on their secret, and then went back to reading the book that she had brought on the trip. It wasn't a Summer Reading Program book like Lulu had brought. It was *Glamour's Big Book of Dos and Don'ts*. It's a big pink book that has fashion tips for women and pictures of people in clothes that say either "*Glamour* Do" or "*Glamour* Don't" underneath them. The pictures that say "*Glamour* Don't" underneath them have a black bar on the person's face, but you can still tell who the famous ones with the bad outfits are.

India read, "'*Glamour* Do: Dress up a casual skirt with a sweater and a blazer. *Glamour* Don't: Don't let a cruel skirt give you muffin top.'" India pointed at the picture. It was a skirt that hung low on a woman's waist, and there was back flab pushed out over the top like the top of a muffin. Mom calls her back flab "backfat."

"'*Glamour* Do: Make a hippie skirt look modern with citified boots.'

"'*Glamour* Don't: Don't show your thong underwear over the top of your jeans.'"

Lulu wasn't really paying attention to India's *Glamour* Dos and *Glamour* Don'ts. Lulu was pulling out her "supplies." A roll of masking tape, a small piece of white poster board, and a set of Magic Markers.

At the top of the poster board she wrote CONDUCT MARKS in big red letters.

"What's a conduct mark?" I asked the manny.

"It's a spot drawn on the ground so a band conductor knows right where to stand so he doesn't accidentally poke someone with his baton," he said.

"It is not," Lulu said in a teacherlike voice. "A conduct mark is a mark against somebody for bad behavior or for not being prepared." Then she wrote all of our names in a column on the left side of the poster board. Belly's name was first and in blue. Mine was next in green. Then the manny, India, Mom, and Dad. Lulu didn't put her own name on the list. She took the masking tape and taped her new sign on the window next to her.

"What's that for?" India asked.

Lulu answered without looking up. She was

marking off a big square around her chair with the masking tape as her personal space not to be crossed. She does this at home, too. We're not allowed to walk close to her room.

Lulu said, "The only way to keep some kind of organization and order on this trip is to make a set of rules and enforce them. I'll make them up as we go, and I'll enforce them. If somebody's conduct isn't appropriate, they will get a conduct mark next to their name as a warning. With every five conduct marks there will be a punishment."

"What's the punishment?" Mom asked without a second thought that Lulu would be in charge of the rules of our trip.

"It's different for each person," said Lulu. "Like if Belly gets five, she'll have to give up DecapiTina for a day." Belly's eyes got big, and she clutched on to DecapiTina's body and kissed the stub of a neck where her head used to be. "And if the manny gets five, he will have to be silent for a day. It's a punishment, so I'm choosing things that will really challenge you."

"It is hard for me to be quiet," the manny agreed.

"How come your name isn't on the conduct mark list?" I asked.

"Oh, I won't get any conduct marks. You

should probably model your behavior after mine," Lulu said confidently.

India rolled her eyes and laughed. Lulu drew a red hash mark next to her name and explained that it was for eye rolling. She turned and looked around, and I could tell she was thinking, *Anybody else?* The manny could tell that's what she was thinking too. He straightened up his posture and put his hands nicely in his lap. Lulu pointed to his foot that was partially on the masking-tape boundary line that she had made. He moved it back into his own personal space and asked Belly if she wanted to sing Disney songs. Belly loves to sing Disney songs.

"NO, THANK YOU," Belly said, looking at Lulu. "HER DOESN'T WANT TO GET ANY CONDO MARKS." Then she waved at Lulu and said, "HER LOVES YOU, LULU."

Lulu took out a smiley-face sticker from her backpack and put it next to Belly's name.

8 Good-Bye, Yellow Brick Road

We had been in the car for only a few hours when we passed a big sign that said VALPARAISO, INDIANA, BIRTHPLACE OF ORVILLE REDENBACHER. SEPTEMBER 6: POPCORN FESTIVAL. There was a big picture of Orville Redenbacher on the sign. It was the same picture that's on his boxes of microwave popcorn. He had white curly hair and wore black glasses, suspenders, and a bow tie. India said that Orville Redenbacher is a *Glamour* Do because he found a look that worked for him and stuck with it. He's famous for making popcorn and for being in his own television commercials. Like the guy in the hotel commercials who says, "We'll leave the light on for you." Or the guy in the chili commercials who says, "Roll that beautiful bean footage!" to his dog. I love that commercial.

I rolled down the window to see if the town smelled like buttered popcorn, but all I could smell was the exhaust and cow poop from a big trailer being pulled ahead of us.

"Ewww!" squealed India as she plugged her nose. Belly checked the bottoms of her shoes to see if she had stepped in anything. Lulu held a pillow over her head until the truck turned down a side road.

A few miles later there was another big sign on the side of the road. This one had a picture of a yellow brick road with Dorothy and Toto on it. In big gold letters it said THE "WIZARD OF OZ" MUSEUM: THE STORE WHERE IT'S NEVER TOO LATE TO HAVE A HAPPY CHILDHOOD!

I was getting ready to ask if we could stop, but the manny beat me to it. "Can we stop? Can we stop?" he begged, shaking his fists together in front of him like he was begging for mercy. He pretended to be overcome with emotion and added, "I'll never ask for anything again. I promise!"

Lulu shook her head and called it "a pathetic display of immaturity." "Pathetic" is the word Lulu called me when I cried because my cowlick wouldn't stay down on picture day at school last year. India said that I looked kind of like Donald Trump in my yearbook photo.

"You mean rich?" I asked, but I knew what she meant.

Dad pulled over in front of a building that had wooden cutouts of the *Wizard of Oz* characters stuck in the front lawn. There was Glinda the Good Witch, Dorothy, the Tin Man, the Cowardly

Lion, the Scarecrow, Munchkins, and even flying monkeys. *The Wizard of Oz* comes on television every year around Christmastime, and we always watch it. Mom sets up sleeping bags on the floor, makes popcorn, and turns out the lights. Up until a few years ago I used to leave the room when the flying monkeys came on because they scared me. But that was when I was little. Now I just hide my head under a pillow until that part is over.

We raced from the RV through the wooden cutouts. The manny was the first one up the porch of the museum. There were speakers on both sides of the doors that were playing, "We're off to see the Wizard, the wonderful Wizard of Oz." India said it was kind of freaky. I'm glad she said it first because I thought it was kind of spooky too. I looked back to make sure Mom and Dad were close by. They were coming up the sidewalk with their arms linked and were skip-dancing the same way Dorothy and her friends do down the yellow brick road in the movie.

"Stop it right now!" yelled Lulu, looking up and down the street to see if there were any cars driving by. Mom and Dad did stop, but started again when Lulu wasn't looking.

The manny and Dad both reached into their front pockets for some money at the same time. There was a sign on the door that said it cost twenty-five cents per person to enter the museum. The manny put his hand on top of Dad's arm to stop him from getting his wallet. He said, "I've got this one covered. You can get dinner," and he pulled out two dollars from his silver money clip.

The museum was one big room with *Wizard of Oz* cookie jars, Dorothy and Toto figurines, and flying monkeys hanging from the ceiling. Even though I'm not as scared of them anymore, I didn't walk underneath them just in case there was an earthquake and they fell.

At the back of the museum was a big red curtain over a blocked-off area.

"Don't go back there, hon!" said the lady who owned the museum when she saw me reaching for the curtain. I told Lulu that maybe the Wizard was back there with his big control panel, but when I peeked through the side of the curtain, all I saw were stacked-up chairs and old rusty bicycles.

Lulu saw the storage room too and started singing, "If *you* only had a brain."

There was a video of *The Wizard of Oz* playing on an old wooden-framed television set. It was at the part where Dorothy had returned home and was pointing at her friends and saying, "And you were there, and you were there." Belly watched it without blinking. When the movie was over, the museum woman walked over to the VCR and started it all over again. Belly took off her shoes and sat down in front of the television like it was our house. She even put her bare feet against the glass of the television set until Mom saw and made her stop. Our television at home always has Belly's dirty footprints all over it.

Dad asked the woman why she'd chosen Chesterton, Indiana, to have her museum.

The woman walked from behind the counter, and I noticed that she had on ruby red slippers just like Dorothy's. She also had two braids in her long gray hair. I've never seen somebody that old wear braids in her hair. Buns yes, but not braids.

"*Glamour* Don't," India whispered into my ear from behind me.

The woman with the braids said, "Well, L. Frank Baum wrote *The Wonderful Wizard of Oz* in Chesterton way back in 1900. We even have a festival every year to celebrate. People come from all over the world and dress up as the characters. I always go as Dorothy. The festival is Chesterton's claim to fame." And she clicked the heels of her ruby red shoes.

Our town doesn't have a "claim to fame" unless you count the streaker every year at the fair. Every year during the final rodeo a man strips naked and runs across the arena with the police chasing him. The audience laughs and cheers, but there are always letters to the editor about it in the newspaper the next week. Lulu wrote one about how nudity is inappropriate anywhere but the shower. It got published, and Lulu cut it out and put it in her achievement scrapbook right next to the results of her eye test: 20/20.

The woman went back behind the counter because Mom was going to pay her for a T-shirt she had picked out for Belly. I suggested to Mom that she get Belly the one that said "Wicked Little Witch," and Mom told me I was being "catty." She told Uncle Max he was catty once when he pointed at her puffy-sleeved dress and told her that the eighties were over. I think "catty" must mean "clever and funny."

Mom didn't buy Belly the T-shirt that I suggested. She got one that said "I Represent the Lollipop Guild" in big rainbow-colored letters. The manny bought a bag of candy corn. Candy corn doesn't have anything to do with *The Wizard of Oz*, but he loves them. I bought postcards.

We thanked the museum woman and walked out onto the yellow-brick-road sidewalk. Belly didn't walk. Dad had to carry her kicking and screaming away from the television. She was pretending to cry, but there weren't any real tears. Mom laughed when I said that she really should have gotten Belly that other shirt.

When we were in our seats, the manny gave himself a hug and smiled and said, "It really is never too late to have a happy childhood." Then he smiled at me, and he had the yellow parts of two candy corns stuck on his front two teeth like big yellow buckteeth. Then he added, "I hope you kids realize how fun being a kid is. It gets complicated when you get older."

Complicated is when things are confusing. The manny's life doesn't seem complicated at all. Maybe he was joking.

Dad started the RV, and the manny put in a CD and turned it up. It was Elton John. He started waving out the window at the museum while the music played. "So good-bye yellow brick road. Where the dogs of society howl. You can't plant me in your penthouse. . . ." Belly was still screaming and crying, only now there were real tears running down her face and her bottom lip was pushed out and quivering. She was waving to the museum too.

On a postcard with a picture of Glinda the Good Witch, I wrote to Uncle Max:

Dear Uncle Max,

We just visited the *Wizard of Oz* museum in Chesterton, Indiana. The drive is pretty boring, but Lulu reads out loud to us from *To Kill a Mockingbird*, and it makes it better. I don't know how she doesn't get carsick.

The manny just choked on candy corn, but he's okay now. Mom took away the bag.

Because of the wonderful things he does,

Keats Rufus Dalinger

Dear Sarah,

This is a picture of the *Wizard of Oz* museum. The lady who runs it is really nice. The manny asked her if she sold courage, but she said no. And he said, "Oh, that's too bad, I have to get back into an RV with these lunatics." She didn't laugh. The manny said it's because his sense of humor was too suffocated. I think that means when something is so funny that you laugh so hard you can't breathe. Lulu said it was because it just wasn't that funny. The manny threw water on Lulu to see if she would melt.

She didn't.

Keats

9 Son of a Biscuit

Belly stopped crying after a little while. Well actually, she cried herself to sleep, and she was still sniffling even though her eyes were closed. She had put on her Lollipop Guild T-shirt and had her thumb up next to her mouth like she was going to suck it, but she wasn't. Lulu told Belly that sucking your thumb is for babies, but that's not what made her quit doing it. She quit after India told her that sucking her thumb would give her buckteeth like a beaver. Belly stopped sucking her thumb immediately. Mom says that Belly is vain. She told me that vain is when you care too much about how you look.

"Like when you wear that mud mask on your face to get rid of the lines around your eyes?" I asked her, touching the tiny little lines next to Mom's eyes. She calls them crow's-feet because it looks like a crow landed on her face and tried to scratch out her eyes with its feet.

"No. That's necessary hygiene, like brushing

your teeth," Mom said, slapping my hand away from her face. "Vain is more like when your uncle Max tries on jeans and asks the saleslady how the rearview is."

I've been with Uncle Max when he shops for jeans. If the saleslady answers his question with "Great!" or "Fantastic!" Uncle Max usually buys the jeans.

Belly is really vain. She dresses herself for preschool and sometimes changes her clothes three times a day. The manny calls them costume changes between acts. He said that Madonna probably does that at home too. Belly puts on outfits and says things like, "HER LOOKS BEAUTIFUL," and, "EVERYONE LOVES HER IN THIS PRINCESS DRESS." She even wears a crown to preschool sometimes. Her teacher, Mrs. Read, says that the other kids treat Belly like she's a real princess and ask if they can do things for her. Throw away her trash. Brush her hair. Carry her out to recess.

Belly woke up when the manny started singing, "'Gary, Indiana, Gary, Indiana, not Louthiana, Parith, Franth, New York, or Rome.'" We were driving through Gary, Indiana, the town where *The Music Man* takes place. *The Music Man* is a musical that has a little redheaded boy with a lisp who pronounces an *s* like a *th*. I watched it with Uncle Max once. I pretended I had a lisp for a few days after that. I thought that it sounded kind of cool and cute. I stopped after I told Dad that I wanted "thpaghetti and meat thauth" for dinner and he said, "I tawt I taw a puddy tat. I did. I did tee a puddy tat," like I was Sylvester the Cat.

"You woke Belly up!" India squealed. "You're going to get in trouble with a capital *T* that rhymes with *P* that stands for 'pool'!" That's another song from *The Music Man*.

Mom and Dad didn't care that the manny woke Belly up. We were almost to Chicago, where we were going to spend the next two nights, in a hotel instead of in the RV. Mom says that we'll get plenty of time in the RV and we should stay in hotels when we get the chance. She says that it will help us keep from driving one another crazy. It's too late for Lulu. She's been watching her masking-taped-off area like a hawk. She even got mad at the manny because his feet smelled bad when he took his shoes off. They did smell a little bit bad, kind of like the feta cheese that Sarah's mom uses to make Greek salad with. She gave the manny a warning and not a conduct mark. I don't have any conduct marks so far either. I want to keep my record clean, even though it's only Lulu. Mom says it's because I'm a people pleaser. She says I inherited that from her and not from Dad. Dad has a conduct mark for singing "Come On Eileen" while we drove through the Dairy Queen drive-through. He also got a free Dilly bar from the drive-through lady because she thought he was charming. I want to be charming like Dad when I grow up. I love Dilly bars. The red ones.

We're staying at a hotel with an indoor/outdoor pool and with room service. I've never had room service. I almost did when I went to New York City with Grandma, but we went out to eat instead because Grandma wanted to show off her new shoes. When the hostess at the restaurant asked what name our reservation was under, Grandma said, "Manolo Blahnik," then she shook her foot out in front of her for the hostess to see. Manolo Blahnik is a kind of fancy shoe that Grandma had a pair of. The hostess laughed and showed off her own shoes. They were black slingbacks. Probably Prada. That's what India said. She knows things like that.

The reservation was really listed under "Keats Dalinger." Grandma thought it would be fun for me to hear them call my name out at the restaurant like I was a grown-up. It would have been too, except they called out, "Kate Dalinger, reservation for three, Kate Dalinger. Do we have a

Kate Dalinger?" India stood up, pointed at me, and said, "Kate's right here." She called me Kate for the rest of the night.

"Kate, have you decided what you want for dinner?"

"Kate, could you pass the salt?"

"Oh, Kate, you have spinach stuck in your teeth."

She stopped calling me Kate after I told the waitress not to bring anything with dairy in it to India because it made her gassy and bloated. It wasn't true, but it made India stop calling me Kate.

Dad started grumbling when we finally reached Chicago. It was rush-hour traffic, and the cars were almost stopped on the freeway. People were honking their horns and pumping their fists into the air, which smelled like car exhaust and hot dogs.

A white-haired lady in a navy blue Chevrolet was right next to us and motioned for my dad to roll down his window. When he rolled it down, the woman yelled, "Let me into your lane, you *son of a biscuit*!" Belly laughed and waved at the lady. She was really angry, but Dad slowed down and waved for her to move in front of him. She didn't even wave and mouth "Thank you" like Mom does. Only, when Mom's driving, she usually waves and mouths the word "Sorry." Lots of people honk at Mom when she's driving. Dad calls her a "weaver."

Dad looked flustered. His face was red, and you could see the vein on the side of his head that comes out when he has a bad day at work or during tax season. I saw the vein once when Belly had taken all the toilet paper in our house and thrown it into the trees to make a pretend winter wonderland. When he sent Belly to her room, she screamed, "YOU'RE NOT HER FRIEND ANYMORE!" and slammed her door so hard that it shook the pictures on the walls. She didn't even come down for dinner. She fell asleep early and didn't wake up until the next morning. It was like I was the youngest in the family again. Mom even read *Goodnight Moon* to me before I went to bed like she used to when I was little.

The traffic was moving so slowly that I could see the people in their cars. One man in a silver Mercedes was reading the newspaper while he was driving. A car full of businessmen passed by with all of them on their cell phones, probably talking about stocks and bonbons. A red-haired lady in a Suburban drove past with five golden retrievers hanging out of the windows. She must really love dogs, because even her license plate said WOOF. She was singing really loudly to a

song about being born to run. The manny rec-
ognized the song and said it was by the Boss.

"The boss of what?" I asked.

He didn't know.

The hotel was right off the interstate. Dad
stretched his arms above his head and let out a
big sigh. The vein faded away and his wrinkled
forehead smoothed out. Dad parked, and Mom
got out to go check into the hotel. Belly and I
were too excited to stay in the RV, so we went in
with her, trying to see the indoor/outdoor swimming pool. I held Belly's hand so the woman at
the front desk would think we were cute. Belly
and I have gotten good at being cute. On air-
planes, when the flight attendants think you're
cute, they give you wing pins or extra peanuts.
At restaurants they bring you a box of crayons
or a crown for your head. At banks they give you
those little Dum Dum suckers. I always hold my
Dum Dum sucker up next to Belly and say,
"You're such a dum-dum!" and then I claim to
be talking to my sucker and not to Belly. She
whines to Mom anyway.

The hotel woman looked at us from behind
the front desk and smiled while Mom signed
some papers. I think she thought we were cute,
because after she told Mom what rooms we
would be in, she held a bowl of candy down for

Belly and me to reach. It was the kind of candy that India calls "grandmother candy." She says that grandmothers don't usually have Swedish Fish or Sour Patch Kids in their purses. They usually have Brach's red-and-white peppermints and yellow butterscotches, the kind that you scoop out of bins and put into little sacks at the grocery store. I took two butterscotch candies from the bowl, one for me and one for the manny. I made it look like I had taken only one by putting my whole hand over the bowl instead of using just my fingers. The lady didn't notice. Mom would have noticed if she had been paying attention. She notices everything.

Last year Mom even noticed when I tweezed my eyebrows. I saw a guy get his eyebrows tweezed on a makeover show on television. Someone showed him how to shape his eyebrows. He called it "contouring." They also made him get his back waxed because he looked like he was getting attacked by squirrels. I hope I never have to get my back waxed. Tweezing my eyebrows hurt bad enough, and the guy screamed and almost started crying when they ripped the wax off his back. He did look better, though. Red and rashy, but better.

Belly took a peppermint from the front-desk woman's bowl. She winked at the woman and said, "THANKS, *SON OF A BISCUIT*!" Mom nearly signed her name all the way off the paper and onto the desktop.

"Belly! Don't talk that way!" Mom said with her "stern look." That's what Lulu calls it when Mom arches her eyebrows and purses her lips. Belly kept smiling at the lady like they were long-lost best friends. She even twinkled her eyes at her. She didn't know that there was anything wrong with what she had said.

The woman behind the front desk looked shocked, like she might put her hand up to her chest and say something like "Oh my" or "Why, I never," but she didn't say anything. She just put the bowl back where it belonged and frowned at me like we weren't as cute as she first thought. Belly was still kind of cute, though. She had licked the peppermint and stuck it on her forehead. The manny taught her that trick.

Mom mouthed the words "I'm sorry" to the woman, just like she does when she's driving, and we walked out of the front doors to go get our luggage. When I looked back at the woman at the front desk, she smiled a fake smile at me, and her glasses were down half of her nose like she might call the police or the Department of Family Services when we were gone. They always call the Department of Family Services on the crime shows on television when the parents have to go to jail.

I clenched my palm to hide the two pieces of candy.

When I gave the manny his butterscotch candy, he licked it and stuck it on his forehead, just like Belly had done. I put my piece in the front pocket of my jeans to save for later. I love a hard candy after a meal. It cleanses the palate. I heard someone say that once.

In the hotel room there were two postcards with a picture of the hotel on them. There was also a Chicago fact sheet that I copied onto Uncle Max's postcard.

Dear Uncle Max,

Chicago is right next to Lake Michigan.

The average temperature is 49.8 degrees.

It gets an average of 33.18 inches of precipitation a year.

Remember how Lulu wouldn't go to the bathroom at home because she didn't want to lose her seat? We stopped for her to go at a gas station, and when she got back to the RV, we were all stacked up in her seat on one another's laps.

Dad, the manny, Mom, India, me, and Belly. It was so funny that we all had to go in and use the restroom.

. . . And all that jazz,

Keats Rufus Dalinger

Dear Sarah,

You can swim inside and outside in the same pool at our hotel. You just have to swim under a wall. It's so cool. The manny swam with us. Lulu was scared because when he went to get ready, he said, "Let me go put on my Speedo!" But he didn't wear a Speedo. He wore red swim trunks. We ordered room service for dinner, and then we ordered chocolate malts as a late-night snack. My stomach kind of hurts. I love vacation.

The manny says tomorrow he's going to try to meet Oprah. She lives here, and the manny says he wants to marry her. Don't tell Uncle Max.

Keats

Chicago is a busy city with lots of museums, parks, and shops. The sound of car horns is all you can hear, and at night you can't see any stars, only blackness above the tall buildings. Mom and Dad looked through a copy of *Chicago* magazine that was in the hotel room to decide what we should do. Dad kept suggesting things like baseball games and history museums. Lulu and the manny really wanted to go see a taping of the Oprah show. I watched an Oprah show with Mom after school once, and Oprah gave away new cars to everyone in the audience. She jumped up and down, pointed to people in the audience, and yelled, "You get a car! You get car! You get a car!" about a hundred times. The audience was screaming, and one lady was crying and shaking like she was having a nervous breakdown, the same way Belly cries and dry-heaves when she doesn't get her way. At dinner that night Mom was imitating Oprah by pointing to each of us and saying, "You get a taco! You get a taco! You get a taco!" India screamed and pretended to be faint with excitement over her taco. They were good, too. Mom used taco seasoning.

The manny looked up the number for Oprah tickets and called, but they weren't taping because Oprah was on "holiday." That's what the lady on the phone told the manny. She called it holiday instead of vacation. The manny said that holidays are the same thing as vacations except you take a private jet and get seaweed body wraps and hot stone massages. I want to go on a holiday.

"I bet Oprah is in Africa building schools to empower girls and women," said Lulu.

"I bet she's off with Nate the decorator shopping for antique chandeliers in Paris," said India.

"Or she and Stedman are in Santa Barbara playing doubles tennis with John Travolta and Kelly Preston," said the manny. Stedman is Oprah's boyfriend. He's really tall and has a mustache. If I ever get a cat, I'm going to name it Stedman.

Since we couldn't get tickets to the Oprah show, we took the hotel shuttle to the Museum of Contemporary Art. Mom read in *Chicago* magazine that there was an Andy Warhol exhibition at the museum. The manny wanted to see it too. I wanted to go just so I could get some Andy Warhol postcards. Uncle Max would think that was cool, and it might inspire some of his paintings for his show.

The museum was crowded with people. Kids from summer day camps. Japanese tourists from buses. Ladies with matching pastel shoes and purses. The ladies weren't really looking at the art. They were talking to one another about skincare products and their kids who were home from college. I heard one lady say that her son was studying to become a Podiatrist. A Podiatrist fixes iPods.

We walked around the museum and tried to keep Belly from touching things. Mom told her that if she was really good in the museum, she could choose what we did that afternoon. We all got worried looks on our faces, even Dad. India said that Belly would probably make us all go back to the hotel to have a pretend tea party. Lulu said that we'd probably all end up skinny-dipping in the hotel swimming pool if Belly got her way.

"Oooh, fun! I love skinny-dipping!" said the manny.

Lulu rolled her eyes.

I looked around to see if anybody had heard

the manny talk about skinny-dipping. Sometimes I wish he would use his inside voice. Not everybody gets his sense of humor.

I didn't want Belly to pick our activity, so I kept a close eye on her, ready to point out anything that she might be doing wrong. I thought it would be easy because Belly is always doing something wrong. One time she glued both her hands to our dining-room table with Dad's Krazy Glue. But Belly didn't do anything wrong at the museum. In fact, she was even trying her hardest to do everything right. She picked up a program and handed it to an older woman who had dropped it. The woman thanked her and said, "Bless your heart."

Belly called the museum security guard "sweetie."

She even turned to a woman who was admiring a painting called *Aorta* by an artist named Julian Schnabel and said, "PRETTY." She said it with her eyes closed, like the beauty of the painting was too much to take in.

The woman was startled because of Belly's loud foghorn voice but said, "It really is, young lady." Then she turned to Dad and said, "What a precocious little girl." I asked India if "precocious" meant the same thing as "obnoxious." She told me that "precocious" meant "wise beyond your age." Belly is not precocious. A precocious girl wouldn't ride an escalator ten times in a row like it was a carnival ride. Belly did that at the mall last winter when we went shopping for the manny's birthday present. We got him sunscreen especially made for bald heads. I picked it out.

The woman walked away, and I turned to Belly and said, "Do you really think this painting is pretty?"

She said to me in an annoyed voice, "NO! HER WAS BEING GOOD, STUPID!" I looked around to see if Mom or Dad had heard her. We're not allowed to call one another stupid or say "Shut up."

They hadn't heard her.

"Shut up!" I said to Belly. Mom looked over like she had heard me, so I looked up at the Julian Schnabel painting and pretended to be admiring the clumps of red paint. I even put my finger on my chin and said, "Hmm," like I was deep in thought about why Schnabel had chosen to paint a big, messy heart. Maybe he had just had his heart broken.

I know who Julian Schnabel is because Grandma had a big book of his paintings at her house. He does really big paintings. Some of them are on broken dishes that are glued onto big boards. My favorite painting by him looks like a headboard of a bed and says THE TEDDY

BEARS PICNIC on it. Grandma gave her copy of the book to Uncle Max before she died. Now it's on Uncle Max's coffee table next to a yellow bowl that I made for him in pottery class. It has my initials carved into the bottom: KRD.

Belly clenched her fists and shouted, "Yesssss!" when Mom told her she had been good in the museum and could choose what we were going to do. It made me nervous because I was scared she was going to pick the Build-A-Bear store. Belly always wants to go to the Build-A-Bear store. She has eight bears that she's built already. They were supposed to be for her friends, but she can never part with them. "BUT HER LOVES HERMAN!" she said once about a scraggly bear with denim jeans and a Western shirt that she had made for her friend Analise but didn't want to give away. Belly loved Herman so much that he spent last winter frozen in a snowbank in our driveway. Housman had dragged him out there and left him there. The manny pretended to arrest Housman for teddy bear homicide. He even paw-printed him.

Belly didn't pick the Build-A-Bear store. Mom listed a few places for Belly to choose from.

"Lincoln Park Zoo to see animals?"

"NOOO," Belly sang.

"Shedd Aquarium to see sharks?"

"NOOO." Belly didn't sing it that time. She said it like Mom was crazy.

"Adler Planetarium to see stars?"

"YES!"

A planetarium is a big dome room that has stars and solar systems projected onto the ceiling. I guess that's the only way people that live in the city get to see stars. Belly wanted to go to the planetarium because she loves stars. She calls them magical. She also calls glue sticks and Fruit Roll-Ups magical. She calls anything that she likes magical.

The planetarium was freezing inside. The air conditioners were blowing, and it felt like we were in a wind tunnel. Luckily, Mom always makes us be prepared, so I had a sweater. It was cashmere. It used to be Uncle Max's, but the manny accidentally put it in the dryer and now it's my size. I told the manny to shrink Uncle Max's green argyle sweater vest for me too, but he said he's not allowed to do the laundry anymore. And then he winked, like it had been his plan all along to get banned from having to do the laundry.

Belly put her hands in her armpits and shivered and said, "HER WANTS TO BUILD-A-BEAR." Then she started holding herself and jumping up and down without her feet leaving the ground. This is Belly's sign that she needs to go to the bathroom. Cold rooms make Belly have to pee.

We can't even go to hockey games. Mom took Belly to the restroom. India went with them. She said she was going to stand underneath the hand dryer to warm up.

Dad, the manny, Lulu, and I went into the Sky Theater to look at the stars. I pointed out the Big Dipper, and Dad pointed out Orion. The manny pointed to a star that was very light and off by itself. "That's my favorite one because it looks lonely and unpopular. I think I'll call it Lulu."

Lulu said, "Funny! *NOT!*" like they do in that movie *Wayne's World.*

Mom, Belly, and India came back from the bathroom and sat down next to us in the theater, and the lights dimmed. India put her toasty-hot hands on my cheeks to let me know that she really had stood under the hand dryers to get warm. Her hands smelled like sanitizing soap. I love the smell of sanitizing soap almost as much as I love the smell of Windex. I also love the smell of Cascade dishwasher soap. Sometimes I put a pinch of it in my jeans pocket so that it makes my hands smell fresh and clean. That's a secret that nobody knows, not even the manny.

In the planetarium I started telling everybody about an interview that I had seen on *20/20* where a woman was talking about how she grew up homeless. "She said that on one of her birthdays she and her dad were lying on their backs and looking up at the stars," I told them. "Her parents couldn't afford to give her a party or buy her a birthday present, so her dad pointed to a star and said, 'That's your present.' She's rich today and rides in limousines to private parties, but the star that her father gave her is still her favorite present that she ever got."

Mom said, "That's a good story, Keats," and she squeezed my hand like she really loved me just then.

Belly said, "A *STAR*?"

I squealed impatiently, "It was all he could give her and it's really all she wanted."

"NOT A BARBIE?" asked Belly.

"No. She just liked being with her dad," I said, still squealing.

Mom squeezed my hand again, but this time it was to get me to stop arguing with Belly.

"WHAT STAR?" asked Belly, looking up at the fake sky, trying to guess.

I didn't answer. Belly makes me mental. Mrs. House used to tell Sarah and me that we made her mental with our "side conversations" during class. We like to talk about who we think will be voted off next on *Project Runway*. Or where we want to live when we grow up. New York City.

As we left the planetarium, a woman in baggy

clothes said hello to me. She was sitting against the building and had a little girl sitting in her lap. Next to her was a sign that said PLEASE HELP.

Dad reached into his pocket and handed her some money, but I was the only one who saw him do it. He walked behind everybody else so that they wouldn't see. The homeless woman smiled and thanked him. I reached into my pocket and handed the little girl my butterscotch candy from the hotel lady.

Dad grabbed my hand and whispered, "That was very kind."

That night I wrote on a postcard with a picture of Andy Warhol with his wild wig:

Dear Uncle Max,

Andy Warhol's studio was called the Factory, and everything was painted silver. Some of his paintings had real diamond dust on them. I think you should paint your whole house gold the way Andy Warhol painted his studio silver. You could even paint the manny. He'd look like an Oscar statue. And you should put smashed jewels in your paintings too.

Waiting for my fifteen minutes of fame,

Keats Rufus Dalinger

On a postcard with a Warhol painting of a banana I wrote:

Dear Sarah,

I like you because you're kind. I just thought I'd tell you.

We went to the planetarium, and it was freezing cold. The manny called it "a tittle bit nipply." Belly is driving me insane. You're so lucky you're an only child.

Your friend,

Keats

I gave a postcard to the manny so he could write one to Uncle Max. The manny wrote on it and then gave it back to me so I could add the P.S. I pretended to be thinking about what I was going to write for my P.S., but really I was reading what the manny had written to Uncle Max, because I'm curious. That's what Grandma called me when I sat behind her during a poker game and asked out loud if four aces was a good hand.

Sugar Bear,

I think your paintings are good enough to be in the Museum of Contemporary Art, and I'm not just saying that because you gave me cashmere socks for Valentine's Day. Your family is nuts . . . especially Keats. I think he needs medication. We're having a great time, but it would be even more fun if you were here. I'm getting nervous about visiting my mom and dad.

Love,

Matthew

P.S. Why does the manny call you Sugar Bear? I picked out this postcard for you. KEATS

P.P.S. I don't need medication. I need cashmere socks for next Valentine's Day.

P.P.P.S. Why is the manny worried about visiting his parents?

I ran out of room on the postcard even though I had three more P.S.'s to write.

Mom and Dad wanted to get an early start because we were driving all the way from Chicago to as far as we could get in Iowa. They tried to carry us out to the RV without waking us up. We didn't even get dressed, we just stayed in our pajamas. I woke up but let Dad carry me anyway. Lulu woke up when the manny grabbed ahold of her feet and Dad grabbed underneath her shoulders like she was a dead body. Lulu told them she would walk because she was afraid that they would drag her across the pavement and get the bottom of her pajamas dirty in an embarrassing spot. India and Belly didn't wake up at all. They didn't even wake up when we stopped at Dunkin' Donuts, but I picked out doughnuts for them anyway. A glazed twist for India and a sprinkle-covered doughnut for Belly even though she doesn't need sugar. Sugar makes her hyper, and Mom says that Belly is "cavity prone." Mom hates taking Belly to the dentist. Belly screams likes she's being tortured even when they're just doing a routine cleaning. Mom's been "referred" four times to new dentists. "Referred" is a nice way of saying, "Please don't bring your daughter back here."

The manny says that maple long johns are his weakness. He had two and a half before he finally stopped and drank his coffee. I had a regular glazed doughnut. I pointed out to the manny that I had only *one* because I have self-control. He said he couldn't laugh because his stomach hurt. He still had his pajamas on too. Striped pajama bottoms and a green T-shirt that said "Local Celebrity" on it in yellow letters.

The RV was very quiet. Mom fell back to sleep in the passenger seat, and Lulu listened to Diana Ross and the Supremes on her iPod. I tried to talk to her, but she hit me in the shoulder and snarled, "Be quiet, I'm listening to my music."

I rubbed my numb shoulder while Lulu sang along, "'What the world needs now is love sweet love. . . . It's the only thing that there's just too little of.'"

I was just going to tell her that her singing was really good, almost like a professional's. When her song finished, she took out her earbuds and asked me what I had wanted.

"What happened to the money Mom and Dad gave you?" I asked.

"What money?" Lulu seemed confused.

"The money they gave you for singing lessons," I said, and smiled. The manny made a *ba-dum-bum* sound, like he was playing a drum for a comedian.

Lulu didn't understand the joke, turned off her iPod, and started reading *To Kill a Mockingbird* out loud. So far India's favorite character in *To Kill a Mockingbird* is Dill because he has a "unique way of looking at the world." Even though his life's not perfect and his mom has left him, he doesn't feel sorry for himself. He still has fun.

After a few hours we were nearly out of Illinois and everybody was asleep except for Dad, who was driving; the manny, who was eating India's doughnut; and me, who was bored out of my mind. Lulu was sleeping with her book on her lap. The manny showed me a fun game called sugar and spice, where you wave to people who are passing you on the highway. He said that they are sugar if they wave back and spice if they don't. Everybody was spice, and we got bored with the game. That's when we decided to make a JUST MARRIED sign and hang it out the side window. The manny wrote

JUST MARRIED in big black letters on two pieces of pink construction paper, which I taped together. I pressed the sign up against the window and waited for people to pass to see if they would see it. An older lady did see it and blew kisses and waved but stopped when she saw that we were a whole family and not honeymooners.

A lady in a white Subaru station wagon rolled down her window and yelled, "Congratulations!" I pulled the sign away from the window and hid it underneath my bottom. The manny covered up his laughter with both of his hands and kicked his feet wildly like he couldn't control himself. We looked around to see if the lady or the manny had woken anybody up. They hadn't. Lulu had her mouth gaping open, and her cheek was all wet from drool. Her book had fallen off of her lap and was lying on the ground on her boundary line that she had made. India's head was under a pillow. Belly was curled up in a ball in her car seat. And Mom was snoring a little. Dad always talks about how Mom snores, but she always denies it.

When we were sure that nobody had woken up, I held the sign against the window again. The first car that passed didn't even notice. They just drove, talking to each other and making hand gestures. I bet they were talking about their feelings. That's the way Mom and Dad talk when they talk about their feelings. Like the time Dad felt underappreciated because Mom was working so much.

Then a big McDonald's semitruck drove by, saw the sign, and pulled down on his horn. *Byaaaaaaaaaaaaaaaah!*

I pulled the sign away and sat on it again. The manny giggled but stopped because he didn't want us to get caught.

Everybody in the RV jumped up at once. Lulu jerked awake. Belly screamed. India's pillow went flying across the RV. Mom stopped snoring and yelled, "What the *hell*?"

When Mom said this, Lulu gave her a conduct mark for inappropriate language. It's Mom's second conduct mark. The first one was for saying the *S* word when she spilled her coffee all over her lap. Mom says the *S* word when she gets hurt or really mad. She is trying to say it less because I started calling the *S* word "Mom's word."

"Ummmm! They said Mom's word!" I said when we were watching *The Sisterhood of the Traveling Pants* on DVD.

Mom's conduct marks will probably all be for language. Other than that, she's pretty well behaved.

The truck went flying by, blasting its horn over and over again. Mom accused Dad of driving recklessly. India said that maybe the trucker saw that the RV was full of kids who would enjoy the blast of a semitruck horn. India always has a positive attitude. That's what Grandma used to say about her.

Lulu said that the trucker was probably hopped up on McDonald's coffee and Egg McMuffins. Grandma never said that Lulu had a positive attitude. She said that Lulu was "suspicious." When Lulu was eight, she used to make Mom taste all of her food just in case someone had poisoned it.

"But what if it *is* poisoned?" Mom asked, wondering why Lulu thought it was okay for her to eat poison.

"I know how to dial 911," Lulu assured her.

Mom looked back at the manny and me like maybe we knew why the truck driver had blared his horn.

"It's a McMystery!" The manny shrugged.

I laughed and made sure the JUST MARRIED sign was well hidden underneath me. Belly said that she needed to go to the bathroom, so we stopped at a convenience store. Mom didn't want to unpack the luggage from the RV bathroom. We all went inside in our pajamas, except for Mom and Dad. They were dressed. Dad pulled next to a pump and got out to get gas.

Inside the store India picked out a bag of Smartfood to buy. Lulu had a V8 in her hands. She loves tomato juice. I tried it once because tomato juice seems so grown-up, but it didn't taste like juice at all. It tasted like cold soup and dirt. Belly and Mom were in the bathroom. We could hear Belly singing, "'Stacy's mom has got it going on . . .'" through the thin fake-wood door. That song is on one of India's *Now* CDs, and Belly loves it. Belly sings when she's on the toilet like it's a stage. The manny says that Céline Dion probably does the same thing. Then he imitated Céline Dion: "'I drove all night to get to you. . . .'" Then he stopped and yelled in a fake French accent, "René plez bring me zum toy-let pa-pear. We are out in zee upztairs rest-room!" René is Céline's husband, who looks like a teddy bear.

Lulu grumbled and followed India over to the glass-door refrigerators to look for drinks. India wanted an orange Fanta.

The manny and I went to the candy section. He picked up a candy necklace and said, "Oh, Keats, this would look gorgeous with your coloring."

I started to laugh and grab a Fun Dip to say, "Hey, are you havin' fun, dip?" when I noticed two teenage boys standing at the end of the candy aisle holding pouches of the bubble gum that looks like chewing tobacco. They were whispering to each other and glancing at us, laughing. I smiled and thought how I wanted to be like the manny because he can even make strangers laugh. Then I noticed that the boys weren't smiling, but were rolling their eyes. They were making fun of the manny. I looked at him. He did look silly in his pajamas, but we were all in our pajamas.

I looked around, wishing the manny could just blend in better and not attract attention.

The manny didn't seem to notice the boys, or if he did, he ignored them. He just stood there in his pajamas scanning the aisles. "Ahh," he screamed. "Milanos!" And he grabbed a bag of Pepperidge Farm cookies.

"Shhh!" I shushed him, trying to get him to talk more quietly.

The two boys elbowed each other and mumbled something about the manny. They stared at him and then at me. One of them said, "What a queer!"

I moved to the chip aisle. I pretended to be looking for a snack, but I was really trying to move away from the manny so that the two boys wouldn't think I was with him. The manny followed me into the chip aisle, so I quickly went into the magazine aisle. The manny followed me. He picked up a copy of the *Enquirer*, pointed at the cover picture, and said, "EGAD! That's the same extraterrestrial that abducted me about two months ago!"

Normally, I would have laughed, but the two boys were imitating the manny, only they were making him sound like a six-year-old little girl with a high voice.

"Egad! Ha, ha, ha!" And they threw their hands up in the air like they had seen a mouse on the ground.

Before I could control it, I blurted out at the manny, "Stop it, you're embarrassing me!"

The manny didn't say anything. He tilted his head back and looked around and noticed the two boys that were flapping their hands. When he looked back at me, his face was whiter than usual.

I fled from the store past the two boys and out to the RV. Dad had a squeegee and was washing the big front window of the RV. I climbed in, sat in my seat, and buckled my seat belt, ready to leave. My ears were throbbing and felt like they were burning red. They felt just like they had the time that I was walking down the hallway at school and a pair of Mom's underwear fell out of the pant leg of my jeans. They had gotten static cling in the dryer and clung to the inside of my jeans. Sarah picked them up and folded them and put them in my backpack. The next day she brought me a *Victoria's Secret* catalog to "pick out what I wanted for my birthday." She laughed until her eyes were watering. I pointed out the lip-shaped cinnamon mints and asked her to order me two boxes.

Mom, Belly, India, Lulu, and the manny walked out of the store just as I reached up to feel how hot my ears were. The manny did look silly in his pajamas. The two boys had come outside too and were still staring at the manny. They had Red Bulls and gum tobacco pouches in their hands. Belly was on the manny's shoulders, and the two of them were scream-singing, "Lulu's mom has got it going on!" I wished the manny could just be normal and not always have to be so funny. But Lulu and India were laughing, and Mom was walking like a supermodel and wiggling her bottom. India calls that kind of walk "shaking your junk." I wanted to disappear but at the same time wished I were out there laughing with them. I can really shake my junk.

They climbed into the RV and settled into their seats. Belly had a Ring Pop on and was admiring it like she had just gotten engaged. She had her hand held out in front of her and was moving it so she could get a look at the big red jewel from all angles. The manny handed me a package of Red Vines and a Country Time lemonade. He also handed me a stack of post-cards.

"I'm sorry I embarrassed you," he said. "Sometimes I go over the top. That's what my dad used to say to me all the time. He used to tell me that I needed to tone it down. I used to embarrass him, too. I'll try to tone it down out in public."

I thought about apologizing, but I just sat there silently sipping my lemonade through a licorice straw that I had made by biting both ends off of a Red Vine. The manny taught me that trick.

The manny looked out the window and opened up his bag of Milano cookies and started to eat one.

"Mmmm," he said in an unenthusiastic, unmannylike way.

12 Dancing Queen

After I finished my Red Vines and lemonade, I tried to think of something funny to say to the manny so he would know I wasn't mad at him or so he would forgive me for hurting his feelings. We were in Iowa, and I saw a green sign that said WATERLOO—3 MILES AHEAD on it. I unbuckled my seat belt and rifled through Mom's book of CDs. I found the ABBA CD right in between Paul Simon's *Graceland* and Guns N' Roses' *Appetite for Destruction*.

I put ABBA in the CD player and turned it up really loud. Mom, who was driving, got it immediately. She rolled down all the automatic windows. She must have caught on to what I was doing. Mom's always one step ahead.

"Waterloo—I was defeated, you won the war. Waterloo—promise to love you for ever more. Waterloo—couldn't escape if I wanted to."

The people walking on the sidewalks in Waterloo stared at us like we were a group of escaped convicts. Mom started seat dancing. She was even swerving a little back and forth to the music, like the whole RV was dancing. Soon we were all seat dancing. The music was so loud that we barely heard the police sirens.

When Mom noticed the flashing red lights in her rearview mirror, she quickly turned off the music and pulled over to the right side of the road.

The RV was completely quiet except for Belly, who went, "OOOOOOH!" like the kids do at school when the secretary comes on the loud-speaker and calls kids down to the principal's office. The kids in my class made that sound last April when the secretary said over the loud-speaker, "Keats Dalinger, please report to the principal's office immediately. Keats Dalinger, please report to the principal's office immedi-ately." The secretary always repeats herself.

I had forgotten my lunch, and the manny delivered it to me. Later, at recess, Craig asked if I had gotten in trouble. I lied and told him yes because I thought it made me sound tougher. When he asked what I had gotten in trouble for, I panicked and told him that I had been caught taking caffeine pills so that I could stay up and study for tests. It didn't really happen to me. It happened to Jessie Spano on *Saved by the Bell*. Craig just looked at me funny and ran off to play kickball. Sarah told me that she had seen that rerun of *Saved by the Bell* too.

Belly was still making the "Oooooh" noise when the police officer walked up to Mom's rolled-down window. Lulu shushed her. She did it so hard that spit came flying out of her mouth, and Belly had to wipe her face off with her hands. Her "Oooooh" turned into an "Ewwwww!"

The police officer had on aviator sunglasses that he didn't take off. His buttoned up shirt stretched tight across his stomach, and his farmer-tanned arms had big muscles. A farmer tan is when you have sleeve marks on your arms from the sun. Dad gets them when he plays golf. When he takes his shirt off, he still looks like he has one on, except for his nipples.

"Do you know how fast you were going, ma'am?" the officer asked.

"She was going forty-seven miles per hour, sir!" I shot my head up between the front seats of the RV to inform the police officer. I had looked at the speedometer right when I heard the police siren. Mom turned to me and glared, so I sat back in my seat.

"You do know that this is a thirty-five-mile-per-hour zone, don't you?"

"I'm sorry, Officer," said Mom. "We were listening to ABBA, and the excitement took

Officer Renny stood at the passenger-side window and said, "My favorite ABBA song is 'Dancing Queen.'"

Dad started the RV and changed the song to "Dancing Queen." We pulled away as Officer Renny was dancing on the side of the road, trying to make Belly laugh through the window. Belly laughed and made the crazy sign by making circles next to her head with her finger.

The manny looked over at me and said, "Nice going, ace! You almost got your mom jail time." He laughed and messed up my hair, which I hadn't brushed yet anyway. I like it when the manny calls me ace. I always call him joker.

Dear Uncle Max (Sugar Bear),

MOM GOT PULLED OVER BY A COP!!!!!!! There's too much to write about it here. I'll tell you later. We're getting ready for bed in the RV. Lulu's been in the bathroom forever. She says she's moisturizing, but I think I just heard her light a match like Dad does to cover the bad smell.

The manny wants me to send his hugs and kisses, even though Lulu says that things like that shouldn't be written on postcards because the mailman reads them.

Hi, Mailman. Thanks for delivering this.

Love,

Keats Rufus Dalinger

After the police officer incident, Dad drove for a few more hours, while Mom stood in the little RV kitchen and made us turkey and cheddar sandwiches with tomatoes, lettuce, and mustard. She called it a "late lunch," but it was more like dinner because it was four o'clock. The sandwiches were really good. Lulu said that it was the best one she'd ever tasted. Then she added that if Mom ever did go to jail for speeding, they'd probably make her wear a hairnet and work in the kitchen. Mom grabbed Lulu's unopened snack bag of Fritos and crunched it in her hands as revenge for the jail comment. Lulu had to eat the chips directly from the bag like a drink. She said it's the price you have to pay for having a quick wit. The manny agreed by nodding. He was paying the price for his quick wit by serving his punishment of silence from too many conduct marks.

We stopped early that evening at an RV campsite that had big marked-off parking places, a fenced-in swimming pool, and a communal bath-room in the middle. There were RVs everywhere. Some were big and fancy and had striped awnings like porches. Some had clotheslines between them with drying sheets and swimsuits. One even had fake green grass around it like it was a yard, the kind of bright green plastic grass that is at miniature golf courses.

We parked next to the green-and-blue-striped RV that had the fake yard around it. An older man in shorts and tall socks waved to us. He was hosing off his fake yard with a jet spray. His wife was grilling burgers on a small grill. She looked kind of like Grandma, except I never saw Grandma wear culottes or a tennis visor. Sitting in a folding chair next to her was a girl a little older than Belly wearing lavender corduroy overalls with a yellow T-shirt underneath. She was swinging her legs back and forth and had a serious look on her face like she was trying to figure out if her grandpa knew that the grass that he was watering was fake.

The manny looked out the window and said, "They really should get a yard boy."

"Why is he watering it?" I asked.

"DUH, SO IT WILL GROW," Belly answered. Belly says "duh" sometimes. She learned it from Lulu.

Dad laughed and brought the RV to a stop. Belly saw the little girl in her lavender overalls and decided she should probably change out of her pajamas. Mom says Belly is "fashion competitive" and doesn't like it if somebody is dressed prettier than she is. Belly put on her Snow White dress that she bought at the Disney Store at the mall. She also put on her cowboy boots and her fake diamond tiara. Mom never should have let Belly pack her own bag.

The man washing his lawn introduced himself. "Hi, I'm Grant. This is my wife, Dana," he said, pointing to the woman in the culottes and tennis visor. "And this young beauty is our granddaughter, Harmony. She just spilled her entire Gatorade on the AstroTurf." When Grant said this, he sprayed the green AstroTurf one last time, and I could see orange Gatorade running off the side and into the dirt.

The little girl in the lavender overalls waved to us with a Barbie that was in her hand. It wasn't really Barbie. It was Skipper, Barbie's little sister. You can tell them apart because Skipper has bangs and tan lines and Barbie doesn't. I only know because India used to play with Barbies and she told me. And sometimes I used to play with her. I was in charge of running the household, cleaning and running the kids to school. India called me Barbie's butler.

Grant shook all of our hands and said, "Welcome to the neighborhood." And then he laughed like he'd said something really funny. Dana called him "a kidder" and offered us chocolate chip cookies out of a square Tupperware container. They looked really good and smelled like butter, but they tasted like refrigerator burn, like they had been in the freezer too long and had to be chipped out of the ice. I didn't say anything. I just ate it politely like Mom taught me. I've always been polite, but Mom says that sometimes my politeness needs direction. When I was six, I went to my friend Elliot's birthday party. His mother made carrot cake. When she offered me a piece, I said, "Oh, no, thank you. It looks wonderful, but it sounds awful." I wasn't invited to Elliot's seventh birthday party. I didn't care. Sarah told me that Elliot's mother made a pecan pie that year. Poor Elliot. I bet his mother gives out toothbrushes or ginger chews at Halloween.

Belly walked up to the little girl in the lavender overalls and smiled and waited to be greeted. That's how Belly introduces herself. She walks up and waits to be talked to, admired, or bowed to.

The little girl held her hand out to shake and said, "My name is Harmony Patricia Draper, and this is Popcorn." Harmony pointed to a brand-new red tricycle. "My mommy gave Popcorn to me."

I've never heard of anybody naming a tricycle, but I guess Popcorn's a pretty good name if you're going to do it. I would have named it Linus. It looked more like a Linus than a Popcorn.

Belly said, "I LIKE YOUR HAIR," and pointed to Harmony's hair, which had about ten plastic hair clips in it. They weren't holding her hair back. They were just clipped in randomly. A pink one was right above her forehead. An orange one was by her ear. And a blue one was at the very bottom of one of her three ponytails.

India said that Harmony's hair was a *Glamour* Do because she was five. She said if Lulu had the same hairdo, it would be a *Glamour* Don't. I laughed at the thought of Lulu with three pony-tails and lots of hair clips.

"What if the manny had that hairdo?" I asked.

"It would be a *Glamour* DOOFUS!" India said, and then she laughed a big "HA, HA, HA."

Belly and Harmony started playing with Harmony's box of Barbies on the fake lawn. Belly kept scratching her legs, saying that the lawn was itchy and asking if there were ticks in it. Belly had a tick on her leg last summer that Mom had to remove with the tweezers. She screamed like Mom was removing her leg.

While Belly and Harmony played, Mom and Dad decided to rest in the RV. The manny, Lulu, India, and I walked around the RV park. As we left the RV, Dad hung out the door and said loud enough for Grant and Dana to hear, "Hey, kids, remember to knock when you get back because your mother and I will probably be making out."

"Dad!" Lulu shrieked, staring at him without blinking, the same way she did to Belly when she stole pictures of Johnny Depp off her Hot Guy Wall. Belly taped them in her dollhouse like Johnny Depp lived there with her dolls Genevieve and Rosie.

While we walked around the RV park, we pretended that we knew people. The manny waved at a man wearing a John Deere T-shirt with the sleeves cut off. His arms were covered in black hair all the way up to his shoulders.

The manny said, "Oh, there's Winslow, bless his heart! I haven't seen him since we used to work at the Rogaine factory together. It looks like his new hair is coming in *extremely* well."

After we passed a pretty blond woman in a red bikini who wasn't much older than Lulu, India said, "Heavens to Betsy, that was Gladys. She looks wonderful for a ninety-six-year-old. God bless BOTOX!"

I spent the whole time we were walking trying to think of something really funny to say, but I couldn't. I kept saying, "Oh, look, there's . . ." but then I'd stop.

Lulu didn't join in. She hates pretending. She calls herself a "realist." India told me that a realist is somebody who doesn't like to daydream or watch cartoons. They only like things that are real. I guess that's why Lulu reads biographies and watches *The Real World* on MTV.

Mom and Dad don't know that Lulu watches *The Real World*. She usually watches it when they have gone to the store or out to eat and they've left her in charge. Mom thinks *The Real World* isn't an appropriate show for kids, even though Lulu is about to go into high school. I saw a little bit of it once when Lulu was watching, and there was a girl sitting in a hot tub talking about how she thought the other roommates didn't respect her. After she said it, she drank right out of a margarita pitcher, took her shirt off, and jumped into the swimming pool. I've never seen anybody in real life do that.

The RV park was like a little town. There were people playing volleyball. There were people eating dinner at folding tables. I even saw a guy reading the *New York Times* in his boxer shorts and undershirt in a lawn chair. The manny pointed out that the man was reading the Style section and said, "At least it's a start."

When we were almost back to our own RV, we saw a little red tricycle barreling toward us. It was Belly on Popcorn, going faster than a tricycle should probably go. Rocks were flying out from underneath the wheels, and Harmony was running after it, screaming through tears, "Give it back! Give back Popcorn! She doesn't like that!"

Harmony had her forehead scrunched up and looked as though, if she caught up, she might beat Belly with the tricycle. Belly just kept pedaling and smiling, pretending like she had no idea Harmony was running after her. Harmony's Skipper doll was stuck in the spokes of the front wheel and was going round and round. *Thwat. Thwat. Thwat.*

When Belly saw the manny, she slammed on the tricycle brakes, and Harmony caught up to her. Harmony grabbed the Skipper doll out of the spokes and said, "I think you killed her."

Belly shrugged.

Harmony screamed and moaned as tears streaked down her bright red face. She was shaking back and forth and shivering like our dog, Housman, does when we give him baths in the sink. Harmony kept sniffling, and you could hear the snot being sucked back into her nostrils. Most of it, anyway. She wiped some of it on her arm and across her red cheek. When she did it,

Lulu looked away and pretended to be distracted by the volleyball game. Lulu hates snot.

The manny picked Belly up off of Popcorn and got a serious look on his face. The manny doesn't get a serious look on his face very often, usually only when he's trying on clothes or watching talk shows. He spoke quietly into Belly's ear. I couldn't hear what he said, but I hoped he was telling her that she was going to be sent to one of those boot camps in the desert where out-of-control kids go. I saw it on *60 Minutes* once. A thirteen-year-old girl had to go to the boot camp because she was smoking cigarettes, dressing in half shirts, and cussing at her mother. After three weeks of being yelled at by a soldier guy with flared nostrils, the same girl was wearing cardigan sweaters, going to church, and calling her mother her "best friend." I think Belly should go there every summer, like camp.

Belly crossed her arms and looked down at Harmony, who had climbed onto her tricycle and was trying to straighten Skipper's new frizzy hair. Lulu was rubbing Harmony's back but still not looking at her face. India was trying to brush Harmony's hair with her hands, but her hand kept getting caught by a hair clip. Harmony was still gasping in between sobs like she was recovering from hyperventilation.

The manny let out a breath through his lips and it made a motor sound. He asked Belly if she had something to say to Harmony.

"YEAH," said Belly. "POPCORN'S FAST! HER WAS SCARED!"

Harmony didn't even look up. She just kept pedaling, with her shoulders stooped.

"No, Belly. I mean, don't you want to apologize to Harmony for taking her tricycle without asking?"

"NOOOOOO," said Belly, adding a few extra o's for emphasis. I taught her that.

"Then, we'll go back and you can sit in the time-out seat in the RV until you can apologize to Harmony," the manny said.

I didn't know we even had a time-out seat in the RV.

"Maybe we should throw her in the bushes. I bet there's a whole bunch of ticks in there," I suggested.

"NO!" Belly screamed, and clutched around the manny's neck with both of her arms. She was too scared to add the extra o's.

"Yeah, throw her in the bushes," Harmony agreed. I smiled at Harmony but had to look away because the snot on her face was starting to crust over.

The manny said, "Hey," and looked down at

me to let me know that I wasn't helping the situation.

"Or the time-out seat sounds good," I said.

We walked back, and Harmony rode alongside on Popcorn, which was squeaking like it needed oil. I'm not sure if it did that before or if Belly had damaged it with her reckless driving.

India and Lulu kept asking Harmony questions about her life, trying to let her know that we weren't a whole family of delinquents. Delinquents are people who wear their hair slicked back and fight with knives. Lulu told me what a delinquent was after she read *The Outsiders* in English class last year. She also told me that the main character in *The Outsiders* is named Ponyboy. Lulu cried when she read the end of the book and said that someday she wanted to marry somebody like Ponyboy because he was "golden." I don't know what "golden" means, but that's how it described him in the book. I wish I had a name like Ponyboy or Sodapop. Sodapop is another boy in the book. India suggested GingerSnap as a nickname for me, but I don't think it's tough enough.

Harmony told us that her mother lived in California at Disneyland and that she's going to go live with her in Cinderella's castle.

The manny said, "Oh, how fun! You're very lucky! I bet you'll get to sleep in a canopy bed, and the mice will sew you pretty dresses." I looked at the manny, and he wasn't teasing Harmony. He was really talking to her.

"I *love* the mice," said Harmony, fake-hugging herself. "They're nice to me when I'm there." Then she sped off on her tricycle and ran into Grant and Dana's RV.

We burst through the door of our RV, and Dad quickly started kissing Mom like that's what they had been doing the whole time we were gone. I could tell they hadn't been kissing because Mom pushed him away and kept reading the *New Yorker*. I looked over her shoulder, and she was reading about a man who could train unruly dogs. There was a picture of him in the middle of a mud puddle, with mean-looking dogs jumping all over the place. Maybe Belly should be sent there instead of to the desert boot camp.

The manny sat Belly in the driver's seat of the RV and explained the whole story to Mom and Dad. About the tricycle. About the Skipper doll being stuck in the spokes. About Belly refusing to apologize. Belly just sat there with her arms still crossed. She kept making "humph" noises. She even told the manny that he wasn't her friend anymore.

Mom told Belly that she thought Harmony was nice and that what Belly did wasn't very nice.

"Harmony's bossy!" shouted Belly as she

widened her eyes and shook her head back and forth for extra attitude.

I thought that was funny because usually it's other kids who call *Belly* bossy. When Belly's friends come over, they play a game called Mean Babysitter where Belly acts like she's the babysitter and bosses the other kids around. She threatens to "swat" them and puts them in the time-out corner. We don't know where she learned the game. Nobody's ever threatened to spank Belly, but maybe they should.

Belly sat in the time-out chair for an hour and a half. She was there when the manny and I left to go swimming, and she was still there when we got back. I made sure to act like I had never had as much fun in my life as I had swimming.

Belly stuck her tongue out at me when I said, "Oh, man, you missed it. Kids were standing in line waiting to have the manny throw them into the swimming pool. You've never seen so many kids flying through the air. It was awesome, dude." I threw in some surfer talk because surfers always seem like they are having a good time.

"It was sick-nar! Totally tubular!" the manny added in surfer talk too. He made a "hang loose" sign with his hand.

Belly didn't budge from her chair except once to go to the bathroom. In fact, she ate dinner and fell asleep in the time-out seat. Mom covered her with her silky blanket, the one made out of her old nightgowns that Grandma had made. Belly slept all night long in the time-out chair.

Lulu and India shared the bed above the driver's seat, and I slept on the couch by the table. I could see the light from Lulu's reading lamp, and she was reading out loud from *To Kill a Mockingbird*. She was at the part where the dad says, "You never really understand a person until you consider things from his point of view . . . until you climb into his skin and walk around in it." Lulu read like she was a book on tape, with a soothing voice and pauses at the end of each sentence. She's a really good reader.

My head was right next to a window that was cracked open a tiny bit because I love the smell of fresh summer air. Or at least that's the excuse I gave. I really wanted to crack it open a little because I wanted to eavesdrop. That's how I found out where babies come from. I heard Mom talking to India about it. I was in the hallway with my notepad, writing it all down like in *Harriet the Spy*. Sarah and I both did book reports on *Harriet the Spy* this year. Sarah got an A. I got a B because I included a list of things I had overheard and written down in a spiral notebook just like Harriet had done in the book. Mrs. House didn't like the list because there was a quote from her when she was talking to Mrs. Grant on the playground and they didn't know I was eavesdropping. The quote was "I'm so glad it's Friday. I sure could use a drink." I thought the list would get me extra credit, but when she returned my paper, the list had been ripped off. I don't know what she did with it. Maybe it's in a scrapbook of excellent student work at her house.

Harmony's grandpa has a portable fire pit, and all the adults were sitting around it. Mom and Dad were snuggled together like somebody was telling ghost stories. The manny had a blanket around his shoulders. He jumped up and screamed like he was on fire when the fire popped, and I had to cover my laughter so they wouldn't know I was still awake. I've gotten really good at eavesdropping. It doesn't even make me have to pee anymore.

As the smell of smoke seeped through the tiny crack in the window, I could hear Harmony's grandpa talking. My head was covered with a sleeping bag except for one of my ears.

"She's been living with us for about a year while her mother tries to get her life in order. Usually she does pretty well, and we do our best to give her a normal childhood, but it's difficult. She's seen so many awful things already."

I tried to get my ear closer to the cracked

window so I could figure out who they were talking about, but I didn't want to get caught like I had when I listened in on Lulu's telephone conversation with Fletcher, a boy from Lulu's class that she "like-likes." The conversation where he asked Lulu to go with him. They didn't really go anywhere. It just means that they're boyfriend/girlfriend and they pass notes in the hallway between classes.

Harmony's grandpa continued, "Her mother named her Harmony because she thought that a new baby would change her life and make it better." They were talking about Harmony. I took my whole head out from under the sleeping bag but kept my eyes closed and pretended to be sleeping.

"And it did for a while . . . but then . . ." He kept pausing like he didn't know what he was going to say next or like he had forgotten.

Dana put her hand on Grant's leg and interjected, "It's just so hard to watch your daughter get so sad and out of control. I can't imagine what it must be like for Harmony seeing it happen to her mother." Then there was complete silence. I opened one eye and peeked out from under the blanket. I could see that Dana had her hands covering her face and was crying.

Grant rubbed her back and looked at Mom, Dad, and the manny and whispered something. I could barely hear him: "Harmony's mother is a math addict. She's getting help, but it's always a struggle. It's very dangerous and takes control of your entire life. At this point we're just planning on raising Harmony ourselves." He got quieter and quieter, and then I couldn't hear anything until Mom, Dad, and the manny walked into the RV and got ready for bed. I still pretended to be asleep when Mom leaned over, brushed the hair away, and kissed me on the forehead.

I couldn't fall asleep. A math addict? How does somebody get addicted to math? I imagined Harmony's mother traveling across the country, neglecting or even forgetting all about Harmony while she was searching for long-division problems to solve. Sarah might have a problem. Last year in Mrs. House's class, when we were practicing multiplication with flash cards, she stood up and yelled, "WRONG!" whenever somebody answered a problem wrong. Then she did a little dance like football players do when they make a touchdown.

Dana was really upset. I think I must have misunderstood her, because I don't think she would be this sad if her daughter just had a problem with math. I thought about asking the manny in the morning, but then he'd know I was eavesdropping. I fell asleep thinking about Harmony and how she doesn't get to live with her mother in Cinderella's castle.

14 Harmony's My BFF

Belly was the first to wake up the next morning. She was still in the driver's seat and figured that she was still in trouble, so she didn't get out of it. Instead she honked the horn of the RV and yelled, "MAAAWM! I NEED YOUR HEEEELLLP!" Mom grumbled and lifted up her head from underneath the covers. She looked like a wet cat, with scrunched-up eyes and messy hair. That's what she always looks like in the morning. Like the before picture on makeover shows.

The manny lifted his head up too. He looked just like he always does, like a cross between Mr. Clean and Vin Diesel without all the muscles. I didn't think of that. India described the manny that way in a descriptive essay that she had to write for her English class about her family. In the same paper she described me as "adorably tolerable." I had to look it up. It means "cute and fairly easy to deal with."

Mom started to get up, but the manny stopped

her. "I'll check on her. You get some rest. You have some speeding to do today."

Mom grumbled but stayed tucked in underneath her covers. The manny walked to the front of the RV to take care of Belly. Along the way he shook my foot and whisper-sang, "Schoolboy, time to wake up and go to school and learn something so you can grow up and be somebody," even though it was summer and I wasn't going to school.

The manny was wearing Uncle Max's black Basquiat T-shirt, which had a white crown on the front. Jean-Michel Basquiat is another artist that Uncle Max likes. His paintings look like graffiti, and they have lots of words on them. Uncle Max met him once in New York City in the 1980s before he died of addiction. He was addicted to drugs, and it ended up killing him. I think Harmony's mother is addicted to drugs.

Belly looked up at the manny, crossed her arms, and said, "YOU'RE NOT HER FRIEND ANYMORE."

Belly is good at holding grudges. She didn't talk to me for a week one time when I wouldn't take her to school as my show-and-tell. She really wanted me to because she had a new dress, but I took a peacock feather instead. I found it in our yard, but I'm pretty sure that it wasn't from a wild peacock. I've never seen a wild peacock in our neighborhood, or anywhere else. I think the feather blew over from Mrs. Waycott's porch. Belly finally started talking to me when I let her wear the peacock feather to preschool. She duct-taped it to the back of her jeans and wore it like a tail all day.

The manny sat down and started talking to Belly, who was staring out the window and pretending not to hear him.

The manny said, "Hey, Belly. I know that you think you were just having fun, but you really hurt Harmony's feelings. Popcorn is very special to her because her mother gave it to her as a present. Harmony is not as lucky as you are. You get to see your mother every day, and Harmony doesn't, so think about how special that tricycle is to her. Imagine if somebody took DecapiTina away from you. Okay?"

Belly didn't answer. She just looked out the window.

"Okay?" he asked her again, only louder to make sure she understood.

"OKAY!" she answered back, kicking the steering wheel.

"Think about what it's like to walk around in Harmony's skin," I said, remembering Lulu's reading from *To Kill a Mockingbird*. Belly looked at me like I was crazy. "Maybe Harmony has a sad life, and Grant and Dana are trying to make it happy. Maybe Popcorn is really special to her. Imagine what it's like to be her. She doesn't get to see her mommy," I added, trying to make sense to Belly.

The manny looked at me, and I stopped talking because I didn't want to give it away that I had eavesdropped.

We were all awake now, and Mom was making us toast. Harmony was playing with her Barbies on the fake lawn around Grant and Dana's RV. She had the Barbies stacked all over Popcorn and was pretending that they were in a beauty pageant.

Belly rolled down the window and said, "Sorry, Harmony."

"Okay," said Harmony like she didn't remember that anything had happened. "Do you want to play beauty pageant?"

Belly climbed out of the window without opening the door. Harmony pushed Popcorn over for Belly to climb down on. They played beauty pageant until the RV was all packed up and Mom and Dad and the manny were saying good-bye to Grant and Dana and giving them hugs and exchanging addresses. I hugged Dana too, a really tight squeeze.

When Dana hugged the manny, she said, "Just give your parents time, they'll come around. Parents love their kids no matter what." The manny squeezed Dana on the shoulder while they hugged. I must have missed some of their conversation around the fire. Harriet the spy would never miss anything.

Belly and Harmony cried when they said good-bye. They held on to each other like they were long-lost sisters, hugging each other and pressing their cheeks together. Just like the girls do in the movie *The Color Purple* when they're being split apart. Lulu had to watch *The Color Purple* for school and write a paper comparing it to a book she read called *Their Eyes Were Watching God*. She got an award for her paper. A gift certificate to an office supply store. She used the gift certificate to buy a frame for her award.

"NO!" Belly wailed. "HARMONY'S MY BFF." India taught Belly that "BFF" means "best friend forever." All of India's friends wrote "BFF" in her yearbook next to their pictures. One girl named Jane didn't write "BFF." She wrote "LYLAS" by her picture. "LYLAS" means, "love you like a sister." Jane comes over to our house for sleepovers sometimes. Jane likes to bake cakes and make prank phone calls to boys. She calls the boys from her class to order pizzas or to say things like "Jane's bakery! We have nice buns!" The manny says that Jane is "hyperactive but in a good way." Like Daffy Duck.

Mom and Dana pulled the two girls apart, and we got into our RV and started to pull away. "Wait!" yelled Harmony, and she ran up to the window that Belly was sitting by. Belly was doing her long fake sob that ended in a dry heave. Harmony handed Belly her Skipper doll and said, "So you won't get lonely." Then she snatched it back, stripped the clothes off Skipper, and handed the doll back to Belly. "I'm keeping this outfit, though, it's really pretty."

Belly hugged the naked Skipper doll, who had a tan line like she'd been swimming all summer in a boy-shorts bikini. Belly grabbed DecapiTina and handed it to Harmony and said, "LOVE HER. HER LIFE IS SAD."

Belly *had* listened to what I had said.

Harmony hugged the headless doll. She rode Popcorn next to the RV for a few feet and then stopped and just waved to Belly. We all waved back.

"I'm really going to miss her," the manny said, too sad to have good posture.

"You didn't spend very much time with Harmony," India said.

The manny dropped his head and said, "No, I mean DecapiTina."

Dear Uncle Max,

Lulu is reading *To Kill a Mockingbird* to us. It's good. I like Boo Radley because he's artistic and uses scissors. He reminds me of you.

P.U. We keep driving by hog farms, and they stink! The manny keeps holding his nose and saying, "Lulu, do you need some Pepto?" She's getting really mad at him. She says that she has never passed gas in her life, but I heard her once. It was really high pitched, like when you let the air out of a balloon slowly.

Your FAVORITE nephew,

Keats Rufus Dalinger

Dear Sarah,

India and Lulu have been fighting in the RV because India thinks Lulu is mean to Belly. The manny keeps saying, "Let's get ready to rumble!" and calls them "WWE." It means World Wrestling Entertainment. Mom says that

we're cooped up and that we need a little space
from one another.

Lulu just glared at me. I don't know why.

Keats

15 She Kisses Boys and Makes Them Pay

The RV was really quiet for a little while, until the manny started teaching us road games. We played alphabet, where you look for the letters of the alphabet in order on roadside signs and license plates. We all got stuck on *Q*, but then Lulu won because she saw a Quality Inn. She also got the *Z* in Sizzler steak house.

We played a game where we took turns singing songs with certain words in them. The manny picked words like "rain" and "love," and we had to sing songs with the words in them. Mom won the rain one because she knew tons. "Over the Rainbow" by Judy Garland. "Rainy Days and Mondays" by the Carpenters. "It's Raining Again" by Supertramp. I'd never heard of half of them. I think she might have made them up.

When we got bored with the games, the manny asked Lulu what she wanted to be when she grew up.

"I am grown up," Lulu corrected him, and then went on. "I want to be a state senator so I can debate and get paid for it."

Lulu opened her mouth to say more, but Belly interrupted her, "HER WANTS TO BE A CHEERLEADER WHEN HER GROWS UP."

Belly practiced yelling cheers all the way to Mount Rushmore. We didn't have to listen to the rest of Lulu's story about wanting to become a senator.

"HER NAME IS BELLY! HER CHEERS! HER LIKES TO CHEER! HER NAME IS BELLY!" Then she went, "WOO-HOO!"

None of Belly's cheers made much sense, and they didn't rhyme, so I came up with one: "Hello! My name is Belly! I have no friends! 'Cause I am smelly!"

Belly didn't like the cheer that I made up. She started doing her fake cry and said, "Keats is being mean."

Mom turned around and cheered, "My name is Keats! I think I'm *smart*! But I am just . . . a great big *fart*!"

Then all sorts of cheers started flying around the RV.

The manny sang, "My name is Lulu! And I don't bark! But I will give you a conduct mark."

India laughed really loudly, so Lulu sang,

"I-N-D-I-A! She kisses boys and makes them pay! Go, India! Hey, hey! Go, India!"

"All right. That's enough," Dad said, looking in the rearview mirror.

India ignored Dad and yelled even louder, "Dad, Dad! He's our guy! But don't tease him! 'Cause he will cry!"

Mom covered her laugh with her hand.

Dad didn't get mad, instead he turned to Mom and sang, "Gimme an *M*. Gimme an *O*. Gimme an *M*. What's that spell?" And then he made siren noises like the police did when they pulled Mom over.

"Hey, nobody's done one about the manny," Mom complained. The RV got quiet while we all thought of cheers about the manny.

Finally I yelled out, "People think the manny's weird! Just because he is a *queer*!" I put extra emphasis on the word "queer."

I laughed at my cheer, but I was the only one. Everybody else was silent, and Lulu even gave me the look that she usually does when she calls me an idiot. She doesn't call me an idiot anymore because she got in trouble from Dad, but she still gives me the look sometimes, and I know she's secretly calling me an idiot in her mind.

The manny broke the silence. He laughed and said, "Hey! That was a good one!"

But the game stopped, and we pulled into the parking lot at Mount Rushmore. Nobody talked, only the manny. I stood close to him while he read a plaque out loud that explained why each president had been chosen to be carved into the side of the mountain. Washington had been chosen to represent the struggle for independence. Lincoln for his views on the equality of people. Jefferson for his belief in government by the people. And Roosevelt for bringing the United States into world affairs.

Belly listened to the manny and practiced her jumps and screamed, "Go, Lincoln! Go, Washton! Go, Rosewell! Go, Jetson!" India and Lulu pretended to be with another family who was dressed preppy and wore sweaters tied around their shoulders.

Dear Uncle Max,

We got to the part in *To Kill a Mockingbird* where Mrs. Dubose calls Atticus a nasty name because he's helping Tom Robinson in court. Atticus told Scout that Mrs. Dubose was showing her ignorance. I like that part because Scout didn't understand and didn't know better, but now she does.

Keats Rufus Dalinger

Dear Sarah,

We made up cheers about one another today in the RV. They were funny, except I called the manny "queer" in one. Mom told me later that the word "queer" is hurtful. The manny was nice about it. I think he knew I didn't know. I thought it would make everyone laugh. They laugh at school when Craig says it. People laughed at Mount Rushmore when Belly pointed and yelled, "BIG FAT HEADS!"

Cheers!

Keats

When we left Mount Rushmore, Dad climbed into the backseat with us while the manny climbed into the passenger seat to keep Mom company while she drove. The manny said that really he was up there to copilot in case Mom got out of control and started a police chase. He said that he had experience with car chases and had once been trapped on a bus that would blow up if it went below fifty miles per hour.

"That wasn't you," said India. "That was Sandra Bullock in *Speed.*"

"Oh, it happened to me, too," the manny said. "*And* I've won a congeniality award in a beauty pageant too. Sandy and I lead parallel lives." Then he snorted when he laughed.

Mom snorted as she laughed too. Mom and the manny get along like Sarah and I do. I bet if they were in the same class, they'd get each other in trouble. I accidentally got Sarah into trouble last year by saying something funny. She got sent to our principal Mr. Allen's office because she couldn't stop laughing in class. I had showed Sarah how to cut the pickle. Uncle Max and the manny are always making each other cut the pickle. One of them puts his index fingers together and says, "Cut the pickle." The other one doesn't have a choice and breaks the two fingers apart with his hand. The one who had the pickle yells, "Tickle, tickle!" and starts tickling the pickle cutter.

Sarah laughed so hard when I tickled her that Mrs. House sent her to the principal's office. Sarah came back and said that she would never do anything to get sent to Mr. Allen's office again, because when he gets serious, he takes off his toupee. She said that while he talked to her about respect for her teachers and adults, he stood there with double-sided tape stuck to the top of his bald head. I'm not sure if it's true or not because Sarah has a great imagination. She wants to be a writer.

The manny and Mom started talking about grown-up things like relationships and credit card bills. The manny still owes a little bit on his college loan. I didn't even know the manny went to college. He told Mom that he had a degree in biology because when he was little, he wanted to be a park ranger because he loved animals and dark green, which is the color of the uniforms.

Mom and the manny didn't know I was listening to their conversation. I had my iPod earbuds in, and everybody else was asleep. The manny and Mom didn't think I was paying attention to them, but I wanted to hear more about the manny in case I ever had to write a biography about somebody fascinating for school.

Mom asked the manny what his family was like, and I closed my eyes and inched my head closer to hear, even though I had my earbuds in my ears and was shaking my head to an imaginary beat.

The manny started talking. "They're great parents. They've always known I wasn't interested in ranching and farming like they are. Most of the kids from my school started their own ranches or help on their family's, but I never wanted that. It wasn't that I didn't fit in. I loved playing football, but I also wanted to be in the plays and in the art classes and wanted to visit big cities."

The manny loved playing football? I almost blew my cover when he said it. I almost whipped my head around and screeched, "Football?!" But I caught myself before I did. He was still talking.

"My mother and father didn't stop speaking to me or disown me or anything when I told them I was gay, but it did change our relationship. We *never* talk about my personal life, especially my father. I don't think he's ashamed. I just think that it's something he doesn't know much about, so he doesn't talk about it. I sent him a letter a few months ago telling him all about Max and how happy I was, but I never heard back and he's never mentioned or asked about Max on the telephone . . . and I don't want to force anything."

The manny was quiet for a moment, and the moment turned into a really long one. He looked like he was thinking about something sad. I wanted to make him feel better, but I didn't know how to do it without letting him know that I was listening. When I was sad about Grandma dying, the manny hugged me and said that Grandma was so lucky to have had a grandson like me.

Then the manny said, "It's hard, though, because I want to be able to share my life with them, and I know that they'd really love Max. When I was growing up, my mom and dad dreamed that I would someday get married and have grandchildren for them. Now, I think, they're still trying to get used to the idea that the kind of life they wanted me to have probably isn't going to happen. You know. No big wedding. No grandchildren."

"You could still have kids. You and Max could adopt," Mom suggested.

"I already feel like I have kids—yours," the manny said. "Getting to be a part of your kids' lives is the best gift you could have ever given to Max and me. And we don't have to pay for their college," he added, laughing.

I laughed too, but not out loud. The manny says something funny even when he seems like he's sad. It's always hard to tell if he's really laughing or just trying to lighten the mood. I heard India say that once.

I wanted to rip off my seat belt and jump in the manny's lap and apologize for the way I acted in the convenience store and for calling him a queer. I wanted to tell him that his dad probably loves him very much but is embarrassed about the way *other* people act. Sometimes it's just easier to fit in than it is to stick up for people.

At school one time a bunch of kids were teasing Craig and saying that he had body odor. They kept calling him "stinky" and "BO boy." I pretended like I didn't hear them teasing him even though I knew it was onions that they were smelling and not Craig's armpits. Craig's mother had put onions on his turkey sandwich, and he had taken them off and gotten the smell all over his hands. I should have stuck up for him, but instead I just ignored it and let the kids keep teasing him.

I didn't rip off my seat belt and jump into the manny's lap. I stayed in my seat and turned my iPod on and started listening to "Seasons of Love" from the *Rent* sound track. I didn't want to eavesdrop on the manny anymore. I just wanted to love him no matter what, even if he did wear his pajamas and attract attention in convenience stores and have kids call him names. Mom calls this kind of love "one-conditional love," because when you love somebody, you think they're number one.

I had just finished listening to "One Song Glory" when Mom pulled the RV into a 7-Eleven so the manny could get a Diet Coke. He calls Diet Cokes "DCs." Everybody else stayed asleep, but I jumped up and walked into the store with Mom and the manny. Mom put her hand up on the manny's shoulder as we walked through the automatic doors.

Mom picked up a few bags of chips and some Snapples. The manny grabbed a DC, and I grabbed a couple of Slim Jims to eat while Lulu was still asleep. She says she hates the smell of processed meat and threatened to give me a wedgie if I ate beef jerky, Slim Jims, or those red pickled meat sticks that come in the fiery package. I love those. I hate wedgies.

The manny put his snacks on the counter to pay and then asked the clerk behind the register for ten lottery tickets. Mom asked for some too.

"If we win big, we could go off to Los Angeles together this fall and have plastic surgery. I could get hair plugs, and you could get a full-body chemical peel," the manny joked with Mom.

The salesclerk overheard and rolled her eyes at the manny without a smile.

I looked at the clerk and pounded my fist on the countertop so hard that it shook the three bottles of Snapple that Mom had gotten for the girls. India's Guava Mania almost fell over. The slam of my fist was so loud that Mom was too shocked to scold me.

I yelled, "He's *GAY*! There's nothing wrong with it. He can get hair plugs if he wants! He's still the most fun person you'll ever meet!" The entire store was staring at us. Even more than they had when the manny wore his pajamas into the convenience store.

"Okay . . . ," the confused salesclerk said carefully, like I was a grizzly bear that she was backing slowly away from. My fist was still clenched on the countertop.

Mom paid, and then we walked out of the store. The manny grabbed ahold of me and heaved me up and put me on his shoulders even though I'm kind of big for that.

"Thanks," he said. "I've never been outed in a 7-Eleven before."

Mom laughed, and I drew an invisible heart on the top of the manny's head with my finger.

We didn't win the lottery.

When we crossed the Wyoming border, the manny rolled down the window and yelped, "Woo-hoo, smell that fresh, clean Wyoming air!" Then he put his head outside the window like a dog and smiled really big. Dad was driving and rolled down his window too. The air was blowing so hard through the RV that Mom and India screamed and started gathering coloring books and empty paper coffee cups that were flying around like an indoor tornado. One of the cups hit Lulu in the head, and she pretended it knocked her unconscious. It made Belly laugh, so Lulu kept doing it. Lulu's more fun when she's playing than she is when she's trying to be in charge of everything.

Just as I started to put my head out the window, I heard a big *whap!* The manny groaned, "Ewww!" and pulled his head back into the RV and grabbed his forehead with his hand.

"I forgot to tell you that Wyoming has a lot of

grasshoppers," he said as he moved his hand away from his head. There was a red welt right above his left eye.

"You could lose an eye that way, you know. You should never stick your head out of a moving vehicle," Lulu said, and then she made "*tsk, tsk*" noises like mothers make when they're talking to kids who should know better than to do the things they are doing.

The manny rolled up the window, rubbed his forehead, and said, "Let's turn on the air-conditioning. Freon smells good too."

"Put your shoes on, kids," said Mom. "We're going to stop at Devils Tower before we drive to Cody." Cody is the town where the manny grew up and where his parents still live. We're staying three nights with his parents on their ranch. I can't wait to see where the manny came from. I bet that his dad wears fancy cowboy boots and does lariat tricks, and his mom is always baking pies and starting food fights.

"WHAT'S DEVILS TOWER?" Belly said, hiding under her jacket like we were getting ready to go into a haunted mansion. I shivered thinking how cool it would be if the RV were the Mystery Machine and we were going across America solving mysteries like Scooby-Doo. I'd be Fred. He's the smart one who gets to wear a kerchief around his neck.

"It's the name of a rock formation that reaches straight up out of the earth," said the manny. "It's not scary. We used to come here for long weekends with my parents."

"Whew," Belly said as she lowered the jacket off her head. Belly hates to be scared. On her last birthday we took her to a pizza place that had games, puppets, and clowns. When one of the clowns came over to our table to bring us balloons, Belly screamed, threw her 7-Up at the clown, and ran and locked herself in the bathroom. Mom tried to get her to come out, but Belly said she wouldn't until all of the clowns were gone. The manager had to come let Mom in the bathroom with the master key. We got our pizzas to go, and Dad apologized to the clown, who had a big 7-Up spot on the front of his pants. The clown said he understood and that he used to be terrified of Shriners on their little motorcycles in parades.

We finished celebrating Belly's birthday at a park down the street from the pizza place. From then on when I didn't want Belly to go into my room, I'd close the door and say, "Don't go in my room, you'll wake up the clown." Then I'd look at her without blinking my eyes.

At Devils Tower we watched people climbing all the way up to the top. The manny explained to me that they were roped in, and if one fell, the other one would lock the rope so nobody would get hurt. It looked crazy to me. I get dizzy on top of the jungle gym at school. I always make Sarah go first when we climb back down so that there is someone underneath me.

Sarah says, "You know I won't be able to catch you."

And I say, "Yeah, but you'll cushion my fall," and she laughs.

I bought two postcards at Devils Tower, one for Sarah and one for Uncle Max.

Dad said, "We still have quite a drive. We better get a move on." He lifted Belly up onto his shoulders. She tickled his ears all the way back to the RV, and he pretended to be hysterical with tickles.

"He sure is a good dad," I heard the manny say to Mom. I ran up and held Dad's hand and rubbed his calluses with my pointer finger. His hand was warm.

India climbed into the RV first, but the manny stopped. He yelled to India, "On belay?" just like we had heard the climbers yelling to each other for permission to climb.

India answered back, "Belay on!" and the manny climbed into the RV.

I strapped my seat belt and started to write my postcards.

I wrote on a postcard that had the Wyoming state flag on it.

Dear Uncle Max,

This is the Wyoming state flag. Wyoming is called the Equality State because the women in Wyoming were the first ones given the right to vote, allowed to serve on juries, and allowed to hold public office. I was also thinking about what a good dad you would make because your hands are nice to hold.

Love,

Keats Rufus Dalinger

The postcard that I picked out for Sarah had a picture of Devils Tower on it with a climber. You could also see the snack shop in the photo. I drew an arrow pointing to the climber and wrote "You" and then an arrow pointing into the door of the snack shop and wrote "Me."

Then I wrote:

Dear Sarah,

The snack shop at Devils Tower served cinnamon-covered churros. The manny ate two. Belly stole some gum and had to take it back to the cashier and apologize. I was humiliated.

On belay,

Keats

Belly and the manny slept most of the drive through Wyoming. Mom drove while Dad navigated the map for her. He kept saying, "Slow down! There's a cop." I guess Mom hadn't learned her lesson.

Lulu and India listened to their music. Lulu was listening to "I Will Survive" over and over again. She said that it was her theme song for the family road trip.

The manny said that his theme song for the trip was "We Are Family" by Sister Sledge.

India was listening to Queen. She sang along, "'Fat bottomed girls, you make the rockin' world go round,'" while she pointed at Lulu.

Lulu saw India pointing at her but couldn't hear her because of her earbuds. She took them out and asked, "Why are you singing and pointing at me?"

India answered, "I was just singing along to "'You're My Best Friend.'"

Lulu's eyes smiled, and she put her earbuds back in. India and I looked at each other and laughed silently with our eyes the same way Lulu had smiled with hers.

With nobody to talk to and the battery dead in my iPod, I pulled out a sketch pad and crayons and began drawing a picture for the manny's parents. The manny says that you should never arrive empty-handed as a guest in someone's home. One time when he came to our house for a dinner party, he brought whoopee cushions for everyone. The kids lost interest in them after a little while, but the adults kept putting them on one another's seats and laughing hysterically when somebody would sit down with a big *phhhhh!* Later that night I even heard one go off in Mom and Dad's bedroom and then Mom start laughing. She had put it under Dad's pillow.

I drew a picture of the manny and me on horses right next to each other with cowboy hats on our heads. Behind us I drew big, snow-covered mountains dotted with bighorn sheep. I drew them extra-long, curly horns. India said that it made them look "regal." I think "regal" must mean "ram tough," like in the Dodge truck commercials.

At the bottom of the picture I wrote, "You did a darned good job of raising your little cowboy!!!"

I put three exclamation points at the end and imagined the manny's father reading it with such enthusiasm that he'd slap his knee when he said the word "darned." That's the way cowboys talk in the movies. They slap their knees and say things like "Doggone it" and "Dang me!"

I was just about finished with the drawing when I heard Belly scream, "CANTALOUPE!" She was pounding on the window and watching something run through a sagebrush field by the highway. It wasn't a cantaloupe. It was an *antelope* and two babies. Belly's scream had woken everybody up. The antelope sped through the sagebrush field until they were out of sight.

The manny yelled, "Hay!" and pointed out the window at a field stacked high with bales of hay. Nobody laughed.

He said, "Country humor is an acquired taste, like coffee or beets."

"Or tube tops!" added India, looking up from her *Glamour* Do/*Glamour* Don't book.

"Or nose rings!" added Lulu.

"Or Howard Stern!" I yelled.

Mom and Dad both turned around to look at me.

"How do you know about Howard Stern?" Mom asked.

"I read about him in *People* magazine," I lied.

I had really heard about him from Craig at school. He told me that Howard Stern has a radio talk show that his dad listens to that has naked ladies and midgets as guests. I've never heard Howard Stern's radio show.

"Your mother's driving is an acquired taste," said Dad, changing the subject before Mom could question me any further. He winked at me.

Mom punched him so hard in the arm that he yelped and rubbed his shoulder. We also swerved a little, and the manny put his hands up in the air and screamed like we were driving off of a cliff.

The road was very curvy, and we even saw a waterfall in a canyon. There were two high-school-age boys jumping from the top of the falls and into the water. People do crazy things in Wyoming. The manny said it's because there's not very much crime, so people have to create their own danger. He said those boys were "brave" and liked to live life on the edge.

"WHAT'S BRAVE?" asked Belly.

Lulu answered, "Brave is when you face your fears. Like the time when I skied down a black-diamond run when I was scared, or the time when I went on the roller coaster with the double loop and was the youngest person to ever ride on it. That's what brave is."

Mom added, "Brave isn't just doing danger-ous and scary things. You are brave when you stand up for what you believe in or when you stick up for other people who might not be able to stick up for themselves. Brave is when you are true to yourself and live your life the way you want to, even though other people might not approve or might be mean about it."

When Mom said that last one, she grabbed the manny's knee and gave it a love squeeze. Belly grabbed my knee and imitated Mom's squeeze, and then she smiled at me.

As we drove away from the waterfall, I stood on my seat and pretended like I was surfing.

"Put your seat belt on, Keats," Dad demanded.

"But I'm brave," I whined, and then tried to deepen my voice so that I actually did sound brave.

Just then Mom swerved to miss hitting a ground squirrel, and I flew off the seat and landed on a big bag of chips, which exploded and flew all over the RV. India and Lulu were trying to cover their laughs until they knew I was okay, and then they didn't try to cover them at all. Belly just ate a chip that had landed on her lap. Embarrassed, I got up, gathered the chips the best that I could, and buckled myself into my seat. I guess not everybody is meant to be the tough kind of brave. Maybe I'm another kind of brave.

Lulu gave me a conduct mark for making a mess.

The manny looked at me and tightened his seat belt. He pointed at Mom and quietly mouthed, "Crazy driver." She didn't see him do it.

I sat quietly the rest of the way and finished my picture for the manny's parents. I drew an arrow that pointed in between two of the words and added the word "brave" in all capitals, so that it said, "You did a darned good job of raising your BRAVE little cowboy!!!"

We were almost to the manny's parents' house when a man on a horse came galloping out of the woods and rode alongside the RV like he was robbing a stagecoach. We all ran to the left side of the RV to see. Mom rolled down her window, and I could hear the clomping of the horse's hooves against the dirt and gravel. It sounded more powerful than the clomping that I've heard during parades.

"That's my dad!" yelled the manny as he started to wave. The manny's dad waved back. He was wearing a straw cowboy hat, dark blue jeans, and beat-up cowboy boots. He looked like the manny, only older and with a black-and-gray mustache that covered the top part of his mouth. When he smiled, I could see a gap between his two front teeth, like Lauren Hutton. Lauren Hutton is a model and actress that is famous for a gap between her teeth. Dad thinks she's beautiful, and whenever she's on television, he makes a "grrrrrr" sound like a purring cat. Mom makes the same sound whenever she sees Matthew McConaughey without a shirt in an *Us* magazine. The manny makes the same sound when a Lucky Charms commercial comes on.

"And that's Cochise!" the manny yelled again, pointing at the black-and-brown-spotted horse. Cochise was running so fast that you could see the muscles in his legs flexing. I thought to myself that the manny's father really should have a helmet on if he was going to ride that fast.

The manny's dad rode Cochise alongside us all the way to the house. Belly hung her head out the window and waved to him the whole way. She kept yelling, "HI, MANNY'S DAD!" and "HI, GOAT CHEESE!" until India explained to Belly that the horse was named after an Apache Indian chief named Cochise, and not after an easily digested dairy product.

"OH, COLD CHEESE! HI, COLD CHEESE!" yelled Belly. India looked at me, shrugged, and gave up.

The manny's parents' house was two stories tall and white, with a big screened-in front porch. There were pots of red geraniums up the steps, and two dogs wrestling and playing at the bottom of them. One of the dogs was sniffing the other dog's backside. Lulu hates it when dogs do that. Once when her friend Margo's dog did that to Housman, Lulu screeched and told Margo that her dog was "ill behaved." Lulu then had to apologize after Housman peed on Margo's leg. She was wearing shorts, and he just lifted his leg on her like she was a tree.

The manny's mother was standing on the front porch waving both arms in the air like the girl gymnasts do at the end of their floor routines. The manny's father rode his horse up to the barn while the manny jumped out of the RV and ran to hug his mother. Lulu, India, Belly, and I followed closely behind him.

The manny's mother had on jeans and a light blue button-up shirt that was open a little bit so you could see a silver necklace with a pendant hanging from it.

"Now, *she* is a *GLAMOUR* DO in all capitals," India announced with approval.

"Mom, these are the Dalinger kids. Lulu, India, Keats, and the one with the Popsicle stick stuck to her bottom is Belly."

Belly did have a Popsicle stick stuck to her bottom. When the manny pointed it out, she looked and laughed but didn't remove it. She left it there like it was part of her outfit.

"And this is my mother, Clarissa."

"Like in *Mrs. Dalloway*?" Lulu asked, trying to

impress Clarissa. *Mrs. Dalloway* is a book by Virginia Woolf. Lulu didn't read it. She read the Spark Notes online. She reads the Spark Notes to classic books and then brings them up in conversation like she's read them.

"That's right," answered the manny's mother as she shook Lulu's hand.

When Clarissa looked at me, I held out my hand to shake just like Lulu had done. Clarissa grabbed it and pulled me close to her and hugged me. She smelled like lemons and salt. When I saw her necklace closely, I noticed that her pendant was a glass bead with a swirl of green running through it.

I said, "You have a lovely décolletage." I had heard a man say it once to a blond woman with a low, swooping neckline and a big emerald green necklace on a late-night movie. In the movie the woman pushed her chest and necklace out toward the man and whispered, "You think so?"

The manny's mother didn't whisper, "You think so?" She said, "Why, thank you," while she laughed and buttoned up her shirt almost to the top. The manny laughed too and then looked at Mom. Mom scowl-smiled at him like she was sending him telepathic messages that he shouldn't be letting me stay up so late.

Lulu told me later that a décolletage is a woman's shoulders, neck, and cleavage area and that it might have been inappropriate for a boy my age to point it out. Then she told me that cleavage is the line that ladies have between their boobs. I thought "décolletage" meant "necklace."

I handed Clarissa the picture that I had drawn. She held it up to the light and examined it like it was counterfeit money.

"It's beautiful," she said. "I'm going to frame it and find a special place for it to hang."

I kicked the dirt around, trying to look humble and embarrassed by Clarissa's compliment. Lulu's not the only one who practices reactions and faces in the mirror. I wasn't embarrassed or humble. I thought the picture was good enough to frame too.

"Maybe I'll be an artist like my uncle Max someday," I told Clarissa.

Clarissa said, "That would be lovely," but she looked away and started talking about all the rain that they'd been getting. I glanced at the manny. He had looked away too and was scrunching his lips together.

Clarissa hugged Mom and Dad and told them how happy she was that her son was getting to spend time with such a nice family. Mom and

Dad said how much they enjoyed having the manny spend time with their children and that he was such a good influence on us. Just then a garter snake slithered across the walkway. Lulu screamed. The manny grabbed it and started chasing us around with it. Lulu is terrified of snakes. Belly isn't. Instead of being chased *by* the manny, Belly was chasing *after* the manny. She was yelling, "HER WANTS TO PET IT!"

Mom and Dad kept talking with Clarissa while we ran around the yard. Every time we ran by them, Lulu screamed, "Why isn't anyone helping us? Call 911!" They just laughed and kept talking, probably about the weather and Mom's bunions. That's what Mom and Dad usually talk about with older people.

The manny stopped to let Belly pet the snake. She named it Lola.

"LOLA'S HER BESTEST SNAKE EVER," Belly said as if she had a pet snake collection at home.

I petted Lola too. I wasn't scared. I was just pretending so I didn't miss out on any of the chasing fun. Lulu and India collapsed on top of each other in the grass with exhaustion. They quickly got up when the manny set Lola on the ground and she started to slither away.

Belly yelled after Lola, "GOOD-BYE, LOLA!

GROW UP! SOMEBODY GO TO SCHOOL!" She got the manny's wake-up words mixed up.

Lulu ran ahead of us back to Mom and Dad and Clarissa.

To Clarissa she said, "You need to punish your son, or he'll never learn that his behavior is not acceptable or appreciated. He's a menace to society!"

Clarissa laughed. "Well, when he was little and we had to punish him, we used to make him wear itchy polyester."

"I looked like I was from *The Brady Bunch*," said the manny. "But I *was* flame resistant."

When the manny's father walked down from the barn, Clarissa introduced us to him. His name is Roger, but Clarissa calls him Rog. When I shook Roger's hand, he said, "Hi, guy!" and winked with the whole right side of his face. His hand was rough and calloused, and his fingernails looked like he had been biting them. I used to bite my fingernails too, until Lulu told me that I could get worms that way. She said it while we were eating spaghetti and meatballs, which Mom said was "tacky." Tacky is what Sarah calls it when Craig asks other kids if they'll invite him to their birth-day parties. India said that it's not really tacky, just desperate. I invited Craig to my birthday party without him having to ask. He gave me a

BB gun, but Mom took it away because guns aren't allowed in our house, except water guns.

"My friend Sarah has a cousin named Roger," I said. "He's one of my favorite people. I've never met a Roger I didn't like."

I've only met two Rogers, but it was still a true statement. I wanted Roger to like me. He squeezed my shoulder and started to help Mom and Dad unpack the RV.

India and Lulu went inside the house to help Clarissa make chocolate chip cookies. The manny took Belly and me up to the barn to see Cochise, who was in a pen with a big, fat cow. The cow was lying down and looked like her legs were too small to support her enormous body. The barn smelled like hay and cow poop. There were cats running around all over the place. The manny kept saying, "Hi, Griddlebone!" or "Hi, Macavity!" or "Hi, Jennyanydots!" Clarissa had named all the cats after the characters in the Broadway musical *Cats*. The manny said it was because his mother loved Andrew Lloyd Webber musicals. Except he didn't say "love," he said she was "obsessed" with them. The same way Lulu is obsessed with the school handbook. She reads it all the time to make sure that she isn't breaking the dress code or having too many sick days.

"Why are there so many kitties?" I asked.

"BECAUSE HER LOVES THEM," Belly said, giving a cat named Bustopher Jones a choke-hold hug around the neck.

Roger answered my question, "They just find us! They come to visit one day and never leave because they love the barn. We take them to get fixed so we won't have any more, and then another stray shows up."

The manny explained that fixing a cat or a dog means it has surgery so it can't have kittens or puppies anymore. He says it's the responsible thing to do so they don't add to the problem of homeless pets.

"Oh, you mean spay and neuter your pets," I said, remembering that the white-haired host of *The Price Is Right* always ended the show by saying, "Help control the pet population—have your pet spayed or neutered." I was watching it once and a woman from Kansas won a sailboat. She jumped up and down even though she probably wouldn't be able to use it for anything except a lawn ornament. That's what the manny said. He also said that the woman should have worn a better bra. He said it quietly to Mom, but I still heard him.

Cochise is a paint, which means he's white with big brown and black splotches. The manny says that Cochise is twenty-two years old and that's why he's so gentle. He's really pretty, and he snorts a lot and whips his tail around to get rid of the flies on his backside. Roger had left the saddle on Cochise so that the manny could give us rides. He lifted me up first and then Belly right in front of me. Then the manny took the reins and led Cochise around the yard. A cat named Rumpleteazer followed us the whole way. Dad waved to us, and Mom took our picture. We even went right up to the kitchen window to wave at Lulu and India, who both had aprons on and were practicing cracking eggs into a mixing bowl. Belly made the manny lift her off of Cochise so she could go inside and practice cracking eggs. I got to ride Cochise all by myself. I hugged him around his neck. His mane smelled like itchy, worn wool socks. I didn't want it to end.

When we got back to the barn, Roger was making sure that there was enough water in the trough for Cochise to drink. The manny lifted me off. I rubbed Cochise's nose while the manny removed the saddle and bridle and hung them up on hooks. The big, fat cow was lying down in the shade. She had dried mud all over the sides of her. Roger said he'd meet us in the house; he was going to hose the cow off because she looked hot. I laughed because at school when things are hot, it means they're sexy or beautiful. Roger meant that the cow looked sweaty and uncomfortable. He didn't mean that she had a spray-on tan and was dressed for a girls' night out.

The house smelled like the freshly baked chocolate chip cookies that were cooling on a metal rack. When the manny grabbed three, his mother pointed her finger at him and reminded him about gluttony. It was the same gluttony talk that he had once given to me when I took too much food at Thanksgiving. The manny told his mother that he didn't need to be reminded, and he took a fourth cookie and shoved the whole thing into his mouth.

"You really are a menace to society," Clarissa said, using Lulu's words. She was whipping all of the eggs that Lulu and India had cracked in a big metal mixing bowl. Mom was giving Belly a bath. All of the eggs she had cracked had ended up in her hair. The manny called her egghead.

I walked around the living room, looking at all of the framed photographs. There was a picture of the manny's nephew wearing only a diaper and cowboy boots. There was a picture of the manny at the county fair when he was little, with no front teeth, wearing a Western shirt. There was a picture of the manny and Uncle Max from their vacation to Palm Springs. They stayed at a hotel called the Parker Palm Springs. Uncle Max told me that a guy named Jonathan Adler designed it. The staff all wore bright pink blazers, and there were chairs that hung from the ceiling like tree swings. Uncle Max has a book by Jonathan Adler that has him on the cover in bright flip-flops sitting in a lime green room. I love looking at it because it gives tips on how to live fabulously.

1. Overtip.
2. Go barefoot.
3. Take tambourine lessons.

The shelf below the picture shelf was full of videos. Most of them were Andrew Lloyd Webber musicals on DVD: *Phantom of the Opera. Evita. Sunset Boulevard.* I picked up *Cats* and looked at the back cover. There was a picture of a human dressed up as a cat singing and looking up into the stage lights that were supposed to look like the moon. Clarissa said that Lulu, India, and I could watch it. Lulu didn't want to. She said she needed some "me time." That's what she says when she wants to be alone. Or sometimes she says, "I have one nerve left, and you're on it!"

Lulu went to the room that she and India were sharing to read. Lulu told her that I reminded her of Scout because I always ask too many questions and I'm a pest. Those are her words, not mine. I like to say that I'm inquisitive. "Inquisitive" means that you ask good questions. That's what Mr. Allen, the principal of our school, called me when I asked him if he made more money than the teachers. He didn't answer me. He just patted me on the head and jangled the change in his front pocket.

India and I settled into beanbag chairs and started watching *Cats*. Belly came out from her bath, already in her pajamas, and joined us at the part where the cats run all around the stage and sing, "Jellicle songs for Jellicle cats, Jellicle songs for Jellicle cats, Jellicle songs for Jellicle cats!" They sing the same line over and over again but stress a different word each time. The manny says it's not brilliant songwriting but it's catchy, like "I like big butts and I cannot lie!" That's another catchy song.

Mom and Dad helped Clarissa with dinner while we watched the rest of the musical. Belly took her shirt off and used it as a pillow. Roger came in and watched the show with us while he drank a beer out of a bottle and ate popcorn. He called it an appetizer. When the movie was over, Belly climbed up on top of Roger's shoulders and started pawing at his head like a cat. She even licked the top of his head like she was cleaning him. He was saved when Clarissa called us in for dinner.

We didn't sit down at the table all at once to eat because we were having made-to-order omelets. There were bowls of cheese, onions, peppers, bacon, ham, tomatoes, cream cheese, and even avocados. Lulu and India took orders on little notepads like they were real waitresses at a diner. They even had on name tags. India's said FLO, and Lulu's said ALICE. Clarissa had a name tag that said MARGE, and Roger kept calling her "Marge in charge." When he did this, she swatted him on the butt with the spatula.

Roger, Dad, and Mom ordered the same thing, Denver omelets, with ham, peppers, onions, and cheddar cheese. Belly ordered a cream cheese omelet and a saucer of milk so she could drink like a cat. The manny ordered a cheddar omelet with avocados and tomatoes. After he ordered it from India, he said, "Why, yer the prettiest little gal I've seen in this joint in some time!"

India turned around to him and put her hand on her hip and said, "Kiss my grits!" in a twangy accent just like the manny told her to.

I ordered a suicide omelet. It's kind of like a suicide soda, where you put a little bit of every kind of soda in your drink at the soda fountain. I did it once at Pizza Hut. It was really gross because it had iced tea, Dr Pepper, and Hi-C fruit punch in it. I got a large, and my dad made me drink every bit of it to teach me a lesson about being wasteful. I threw up in his car on the way home. Mom said I taught him a lesson about teaching lessons. There's still a stain on the floorboard of his Audi.

My omelet had a little bit of everything in it. Roger thought it sounded so good that he ordered a suicide omelet too. Clarissa made herself a garden omelet, with just vegetables. She told me that eating like that was what kept her décolletage so beautiful. I felt myself blush.

We sat around a dining-room table that was big enough for twelve people to sit at. I thought that there were so many of us that the kids would have to sit at a kids' table, but Clarissa said that she didn't like being separated from the kids because "kids make conversations more fascinating." At the kids' table we usually compare our scars and talk about who we know that pees their pants when they laugh too hard. India's friend Taylor does. One time India imitated Napoleon Dynamite and asked Taylor if she "wanted some tots." Taylor thought it was so funny that she left a puddle on one of our barstools. I don't sit on that barstool anymore, even though the manny cleaned it with disinfectant.

We didn't talk about scars or pee at dinner that night. We talked about current events, politics, and places we'd like to visit someday.

Clarissa said she'd like to visit Morocco and Vietnam.

Dad said Dubai.

India said India.

I said Dollywood, Dolly Parton's theme park in Tennessee. Craig went there over spring break and said that there's a ride called the Tennessee Tornado that does loop-the-loops like you're stuck inside a tornado. The table got silent and everybody stared at me. The only sound was Belly slurping milk out of her saucer.

"I think Dollywood looks like fun," Clarissa finally said, smiling at me.

Lulu cleared her throat and leaned up on the table, with her hands gesturing out toward her audience. "I'd love to visit Monticello, the home of Thomas Jefferson. He was, you know, the primary author of the Declaration of Independence." Lulu looked around the room, hoping to get some approval. It was the same look that the president gives to the audience during his State of the Union address when he uses words like "resolve" and "subliminable."

"GOY!" I said to Lulu when she was done with her story.

"What does 'GOY' mean?" Mom asked.

"'Get over yourself!'" I said. "Sarah made it up."

Everybody laughed. Even Lulu, who laughed and slapped me on the back like I was a cute kid and she was an adult.

The manny told Lulu that his parents had taken his sister and him to Monticello when they were in middle school. They had also gone to Washington DC. Clarissa pulled a framed picture off the picture table of the manny and his sister in front of the Lincoln Memorial. The manny had blond hair that was parted on the side and was long in back. He called it a mullet.

India said, "I'm wondering if your hair really fell out, or if it ran away out of embarrassment." The manny pretended to wipe tears from his eyes.

"It's okay," India said, rubbing the manny's bald head. "You've turned your *Glamour* Don't into a *Glamour* Do."

Lulu looked at the picture of the Lincoln Memorial and sighed, "Ah, the Great Emancipator," trying to show off her knowledge again. Lulu helped me with a report on President Lincoln for history class this year. He was called the Great Emancipator because he signed a treaty that ended slavery. My report was titled

"Abraham Lincoln: Forward Thinker in Top Hat."
Sarah's report was titled "Dolley Madison: You
Think You Know Everything About Her, But You
Donut." Mrs. House put a red smiley face by
our titles. She even drew a top hat and a goatee
on my smiley face.

"Max and I want to take a trip to Paris—," the
manny started a story but was interrupted by
his dad, who stood up and started clearing off
the table.

"Anybody want to help me with the dishes?"
Roger asked.

I stood up and started to help clear and
noticed the manny look at Mom, shrug, and then
look down into his empty plate. I cleared his
plate and leaned close to him. It must have
cheered him up, because he lifted his head and
yelled, "I get to dry!"

The "ladies," as Belly wanted us to call them,
sat around the fireplace while Dad, the manny,
Roger, and I cleaned up and washed the dishes. I
could hear Mom telling Clarissa about Uncle Max
and his painting show. Lulu and India were playing checkers on a wooden checkerboard that was
on the coffee table, while Belly was petting a
fluffy yellow cat named Skimbleshanks under the
collar. Mauling would be a better way to describe
what she was doing, actually. Mom would stop

her story every once in a while to tell Belly not to be so rough. Belly loves animals, but she can get carried away. Kind of like Lennie in *Of Mice and Men*, another book that Lulu read out loud to us. Lennie is a man who keeps mice in his pocket and loves a puppy so much that he hugs and squeezes it so hard that it dies. Belly has never loved an animal to death, but she once loved a hamster so hard that it limped away when she put it down.

By the time we finished the dishes, it was already time for bed. Mom and Dad and Belly stayed in the guest room, which had its own bathroom. India and Lulu stayed in the manny's sister's old room, which had a canopy bed and lots of stuffed animals and posters of a rock band called Bon Jovi on the walls. I was staying with the manny in his old room. It had bunk beds and red carpet and medals from when he used to compete in gymnastics meets when he was little. There was also a stack of cassette tapes on a shelf: Michael Jackson, *Thriller*; Hall and Oates, *Private Eyes*; Prince, *Purple Rain*.

I climbed on the top bunk and found a stack of Wyoming postcards up there. The manny must have told Clarissa and Roger that I was sending postcards every day, so they stocked up on some for me. I smiled.

On a postcard with a buffalo on it I wrote:

Dear Uncle Max,

The manny seems sad because his mom and dad won't talk about you. I think they would really like you if they got to know you. His dad has the same kind of sense of humor that you do. Warped. He hid in the closet and jumped out and scared Mom. She said, "HOLY —!" Don't tell Mom I told you.

Keats Rufus Dalinger

I wrote to Sarah on a postcard with a picture of a jackalope on it. A jackalope is a mix between a jackrabbit and an antelope. They don't really exist. It's really just a stuffed rabbit with deer antlers glued to its head. It looks like something that might live near a nuclear power plant.

Dear Sarah,

Have you ever seen the musical *Cats*? It's kind of creepy. There are a bunch of people dressed up as cats, and they sing and dance and lick the tops of their hands like they're cleaning themselves. I wish they would have shown them going to the bathroom in a great big litter box. That would have been funny. The manny just made a fart noise when his mom walked by, and then he yelled, "Mom! GROSS!" like she had done it.

From the Cowboy State,

Keats

The manny wrote a postcard to Uncle Max, and I wrote the P.S. again.

Sugar Bear,

I miss your hugs!

Thanks for being you!

Cut the pickle!

Love,

Matthew

P.S. I miss you too, pickle cutter.

Keats

20 Expelliamus!

When I woke up the next morning, the manny was already up and had made his bed. He's really neat and organized. I got up and made my bed too. I found a quarter in my bag and tried to bounce it on the bed to see if I had made it really tight. I saw on a movie once that in the army they make you make your bed so perfect that you can bounce a quarter on it. The quarter didn't bounce. It just plopped. I think it would have bounced if there hadn't been egg-crate foam on top of the mattress.

The house was quiet. When I walked into the kitchen, the manny and his mother were sitting at the table drinking coffee. The manny was in Uncle Max's Basquiat T-shirt again and his pajama pants. Clarissa was wearing a terry-cloth robe that was tied so tightly that you couldn't see her cleavage or her décolletage. She was talking to the manny softly, and I heard her say, "Matthew, we love you dearly, but people around here just wouldn't understand. Your father is having a hard time . . ." She stopped when the manny looked up from his coffee and smiled when he saw me.

"Expelliamus!" he exclaimed like something magical had happened when I walked into the room. "Expelliamus" is what Harry Potter says to get his magic wand to work. The manny also used his napkin to dry his eyes. He wasn't crying, but his eyes were watery. I hoped it was hay fever.

Clarissa stood up and kept her back to me. I could tell that she was wiping her own eyes as she walked over to the stove. "Your mother and father went on a walk around the pasture with Rog. Your mom said that you love bagels and cream cheese with jam." She sliced a bagel in half and put it in the toaster.

The manny added, "The girls are still sleeping."

I ate the bagel with cream cheese and jam. The kitchen was silent, and I could tell the manny and his mother were wrapped up in their own thoughts. That's what Sarah's mother calls it when Sarah daydreams. Sarah always daydreams. Last year during a softball game Sarah missed a fly ball because she was daydreaming. The ball almost landed on her head, but she didn't notice it until the third baseman ran out to pick it up. She told me that she was thinking about how hot the sun was and that it probably would have done more to Icarus than just melt his wax wings. Icarus is a character in Greek mythology whose father made him wax wings to escape prison and told him not to fly too close to the sun because the wings would melt. Icarus was so excited to be flying that he forgot his father's warning and got too close to the sun, and the wings melted and he fell into the sea. Sarah did a painting called *Icarus's Wings* in the after-school art program. She used real feathers and melted wax. I made a macaroni peace sign on construction paper.

Mom, Dad, and Roger walked in just as I took my last bite of bagel.

"Morning, babe," Mom said to me. I love when she calls me babe.

"Morning," I said, and cleared my own plate and loaded it into the dishwasher.

Roger squeezed the manny's shoulder as he walked by to give Clarissa a kiss on the cheek. It wasn't really her cheek. It was her neck, and she squished her head and shoulder together and giggled.

"Ewww!" Lulu squealed from the doorway. "PDA is not acceptable." She walked over and poured herself a cup of coffee. When she sat down, Dad took it away from her.

"You're not allowed coffee. You don't even like it."

"I might," she said. "I have sophisticated taste."

Clarissa and Rog laughed.

"Do you have any Crunchberries?" Lulu asked, forgetting about her sophisticated taste.

Once everybody was up and had eaten breakfast, we decided to go into town to walk around and shop and have lunch. Dad, the manny, Roger, and I rode in Roger's truck. The girls all rode in Clarissa's convertible Volkswagen Bug. It was one of the old kind and was black and shiny.

"HEY, BOYS." Belly flirted through our open window as they drove by us. She looked like she was about to explode or pee her pants she was so excited to be in a convertible. I was glad I was in the truck. Belly gets unbearable when she's excited. That means that she's so annoying that bears wouldn't even eat her.

The downtown had wooden sidewalks and looked like it was out of an Old West movie. I wished I had a metal detector, because I bet there's lots of lost change between the side-walk slats. And jewelry, too. India told me that there was probably also a lot of spit-out gum.

Everybody waved at Clarissa and Roger like

they were the mayors. They kept stopping and reintroducing the manny to their friends.

"You remember Matthew, don't you?" Clarissa said to the sheriff, who pulled his squad car over to talk to them.

"Of course I do," the sheriff said. "Remember when we had to bring him home that one time because he had sneaked out and was still trick-or-treating at midnight on his bicycle. We got so many calls."

"I got a whole lot of candy, though, and some money, too. They give better stuff after bedtime," the manny turned and told me.

They all laughed, and then Lulu pointed out a jaywalker to the sheriff and he had to leave.

The first place that we went into was an old-time photo shop where people get dressed up like characters out of the Old West and have their pictures taken. There was a group of high school girls getting their picture taken like they were saloon tramps. That's what India said before Mom raised her eyebrows at her.

"HER WANTS TO DRESS UP," Belly said, jumping up and down and up and down like she was on a pogo stick.

"I don't know—," said Mom, but Dad interrupted her.

"It might be fun to have one of the kids for my desk at the office."

Mom looked annoyed. "Okay, but nobody dresses up like a saloon tramp."

"Mom! RUDE!" India jokingly reprimanded.

Nobody did dress up like a saloon tramp. Lulu dressed up like a schoolmarm, with a bun in her hair, wire-rimmed glasses, and a wooden ruler like she was going to swat us. India, Belly, and I were old-time students. India wore a gingham dress and had two braids, one on each side of her head. Belly wore a dress that matched India's, and got to hold an old, raggedy doll. She wanted braids, but her hair was too short. She cried, which made the picture even better because nobody smiles in old photos. They just look sad. I got to wear knickers, which are short pants that have buttons around the calves; a plain white shirt; and a newsboy cap.

The manny thought I looked like Oliver from the musical. He started to sing, "'Consider yourself at home. Consider yourself one of the family. . . .'"

The picture turned out really funny because Lulu was really swatting the ruler in her hand, threatening the manny. Belly looked like she really hated school, and India was rolling her eyes, so she looked like the troublemaker. I just looked like myself. Really cute and nice, like I was the teacher's pet.

Dad paid for two copies, one for us and one for Roger and Clarissa to put on their picture table. Dad wouldn't let Belly look at the picture while we were walking along the sidewalk. He told her to wait until we were inside the restaurant across the street. The restaurant had one of my favorite things as a dessert special, rice pudding with caramel sauce. It was written on a chalkboard with pink chalk. Belly licked her finger and erased the *R*, so it looked like "ice pudding." I saw her do it, but Mom didn't.

The booths were red vinyl and made funny noises when we scooted across them. I was in shorts, so I kept sticking to them. I don't think the waitress wiped off the seats between breakfast and lunch, because I stuck in syrup and it was gross.

"The usual?" the waitress asked Roger and Clarissa. They nodded.

"I'll have the usual too," I said, and closed my menu. The waitress looked at Mom.

"Grilled cheese with tomato and bacon," Mom said to her. Then she ordered for herself and Belly, a Cobb salad to share. India and Lulu ordered Cobb salads too. Dad ordered Frito chili pie. The manny ordered a Frito chili pie too.

"Can I change my order from the usual to a Frito chili pie?" I asked the waitress. I always change my order if I order first; it's part of what makes me "me." Sarah says that all the time. Things that make her "her" are eating raw spaghetti, sleeping with her teddy bear, and loving tragic movies like *Edward Scissorhands*.

"Sure thing, hon," the waitress said, before she collected the menus and screamed the orders to the line cooks.

A man with a beard and a woman the same age as Roger and Clarissa came up to the table. The man said, "Stayin' out of trouble?" and then he laughed like he'd never said it before, but I had heard him say it to another table a few minutes earlier.

"Yep," said Roger. "Do you remember our son, Matthew?" Roger smiled and pointed at the manny, across the table. He looked really proud to be the manny's dad.

"Yessss!" the woman excitedly said, like she had lost her memory but now it was all coming back to her. "How are you? I haven't seen you since you graduated from high school."

"I'm fine," the manny said. "You look wonderful."

The woman smiled and then covered it with her hand.

She said, "Thank you. I walk two miles every evening. I started exercising when I started having grandchildren. I have *five*." She emphasized "five" and then nodded her head yes to confirm that she really did have five grandchildren.

She went on, "You remember Melanie? She was about your age. She got married a few years ago to a doctor in Denver and they have three girls, and then my son, J.D., has twin boys who are adorable." She reached into her purse for pictures. The twins *were* adorable. They had milk cheeks. Babies who are breast-fed have milk cheeks. They're really fat and full. I learned that on the Learning Channel, which is the *perfect* name for that channel.

"They *are* cute!" the manny agreed.

The woman asked, "Do you have children? Are you married?"

Roger answered before the manny did. "He's not married, yet. He hasn't found the right person. He's very special, you know . . . holding out for the perfect wife."

"Too late. I got her," the man with the beard said, and he squeezed his wife in a sideways hug while she put away the pictures of her cheeky grandchildren. They told the manny how nice it was to see him again, and the manny told them to tell Melanie hello, and then they walked away.

The manny held up his hands like people do when they ask questions, and quietly said, "Dad?! I have found somebody."

Roger didn't answer because the waitress brought two plates of usuals and our salads and Frito chili pies to the table. I'm glad I didn't get the usual, because it was cottage cheese and a ham steak. Blah!

I stared at the manny while we ate. He didn't notice. It was like he was in another world. He didn't even make a comment when Lulu sent her Cobb salad back because there were more cubes of cheese than there was ham and she thought there should be an equal amount. He did notice me staring at him when the waitress came to take our dessert order.

He smiled and asked the waitress for an order of ice pudding.

"You mean rice pudding?" the waitress asked back.

"It says 'ice pudding' on the sign, and ice pudding sounds good!"

"Somebody must have erased the *R*," said the waitress, obviously tired from her day and tired of customer humor.

Belly covered her mouth with both hands, pulled her knees up into the booth, and laughed her fake laugh, which sounds like a donkey. I ordered rice pudding too and shared it with Roger.

That night I looked at old yearbooks of the manny's. He was voted Class Clown, Best Dressed, and Most Likely to Succeed. In every photo he had his hands on his hips. I'm going to pose like that in next year's class photo. The manny was in his parents' room talking to them. He'd told me that they needed some alone time. I didn't even ask him what they were going to talk about. It was none of my business.

He was still gone when I fell asleep.

The manny's dad woke us up really early the next morning, even before the sun had risen. He poked his head in the bedroom door and sang, "Schoolboy! Time to wake up and go to school and learn something so you can grow up and be somebody!" It was the same song the manny sings to us to wake us up! Then he said in a normal voice, "Son, I need your help, the old cow is having her calf."

"We better go help him . . . schoolboy," I said to the manny.

The manny hopped out of bed and pulled on his jeans over his pajama pants. I did the same thing. They were all bunched up and uncomfortable, but I guess that's just how things are on a ranch. Bunched up and uncomfortable.

Clarissa was in the kitchen making coffee. The manny grabbed a cup, and I grabbed a glass of freshly squeezed orange juice. Roger was already running up to the barn, so we gulped down our drinks the same way guys do in the movies when they get drunk in bars and talk about their ex-wives, who have all their money.

In the garage the manny put on a pair of his dad's cowboy boots. I put on a pair of cowboy boots that had belonged to the manny when he was little. They were red with black stitching. The two dogs were shut in the garage so that they wouldn't bother the old cow. Daisy gave me a pitiful look, and I said to her, "Awww, give me your sad face, Daisy!" I caught myself saying it out loud and stopped to see if the manny had heard me talking to a dog. You're not supposed to be sensitive on a farm. I don't think he heard me, because he was already heading out the door. We were careful not to let the dogs out.

The fat cow was lying on her side, breathing heavily and making noises that sounded like a mix between a moo and a Yoko Ono album. Sarah's mom listens to Yoko Ono sometimes when she's meditating. Yoko Ono was married to John Lennon, but her music is way different from the Beatles'. Her songs have a lot of weird noises and screams in them. They sort of sound like the Halloween CD that Mom bought at Target.

There was a string of syrupy-looking slime

coming out of the cow's back end. Roger called the cow's back end "the birth canal." He was rubbing her stomach, which looked like a big, stretched-out balloon. Mom and Dad had come out to see what was going on. Mom had an afghan around her shoulders and a steaming coffee mug between her two hands like she was starring in a Folgers coffee commercial. "'*The best part of waking up is Folgers in your cup,*'" I sang to myself when I saw her.

The old cow stood up, and Roger stood up with her. She made a big noise into the air with her mouth as her ribs moved in and out, and I could see her fat belly contracting. The manny told me to watch her birth canal carefully because pretty soon there would be two hooves poking out, and then a nose and head. I watched closely, and with the cow's next exhaled breath, out popped a hoof. I waited for the other hoof and the nose and head, but nothing happened. We just stood there for a minute, until Roger yelled for the manny to get a bucket of soapy water and some towels. I followed the manny as he ran toward the house.

"What's going on?" I asked.

The manny answered breathlessly, "I th the calf is breech. The cow needs help g birth, or she and the calf might not sur didn't know what breech was, but it serious and made me wonder if we'd have to give the cow a C-section. Mom had to get a C-section with Belly. Maybe Belly was breech. That would explain a lot.

Clarissa gave me a bunch of old towels while the manny filled a bucket with warm, soapy water.

When we got back to the barn, Roger was searching for chains. He said, "Matty, see if you can find the other leg. We're going to have to pull this calf." I'd never heard anyone call the manny Matty before. It made him smile, and he looked like his dad had just hugged him.

The manny looked at me with raised eyebrows and said, "Are you ready for this?"

I didn't know what he meant, but I said, "Sure am, Matty."

He smiled, rolled his eyes, and said, "GOY!" The manny can joke through anything.

The manny rolled up his right sleeve all the way to his shoulder and rubbed soapy water all over his arm. He stood at the back of the cow and slowly slid his arm into the birth canal. Mom ran inside to get her camera.

Roger came into the pen carrying chains and asked, "Can you find it?"

The manny pushed his arm farther into the birth canal. His entire arm, almost up to his shoulder, was in the back of the cow. Roger held a bucket of grain in front of her to distract her. I couldn't imagine that that would keep the cow from noticing what was going on at the other end, but she actually started eating. Mom had returned and was snapping pictures. She said she was going to sell them to *Us* magazine for the "Stars: They're Just Like Us" section.

"Got it!" yelled the manny with a scrunched-up look of concentration on his face. He slowly removed his arm from the cow, pulling a second hoof out of the birth canal. Roger quickly tied the chains around the calf's legs, and he and the manny began to pull them down toward the ground.

You could see their arms flexing. The manny's arm was still covered in slime and whatever else might be in a birth canal of a cow. It didn't seem to bother him. The back legs and hips of the calf slid out of the cow, and then the front end and then the head. Roger held on to the calf, and the manny took his hand and cleaned the calf's mouth out to make sure that it could breathe. Then he wiped the calf off with a towel.

I hosed the manny's arms and hands off. He dried them and then took a clean towel and wiped his face. When he smiled at me, there was still something dark and gross on his right cheek, so I licked a clean washcloth and then blotted his face just like Mom does.

Lulu, India, and Belly came running up to the barn, with Daisy and Dipper. Clarissa walked behind them with a group of cats following her like she was Snow White.

Roger yelled, "Who let the dogs out?"

And the manny went, "Woof, woof, woof, woof," like in the song.

Lulu grabbed Daisy, and India grabbed Dipper, and they sat down with them and hugged them around their necks and petted them. Dad lifted Belly up on his shoulders, and she made a loop with her arms around his chin. Roger and the manny had cow poop and blood all over their clothes, but Lulu didn't seem disgusted by it. She made an "Awwww" sound and covered her mouth with both of her hands when she saw the calf. She does the same thing when she sees the "New Babies" page in the weekly newspaper that shows the new babies that have been born and still look like aliens.

The new little calf didn't look like an alien. It was red colored, with a white face. It was a boy calf, and when he tried to stand up, he wobbled around and moved like he was stiff, like Bambi did when he first tried to walk. The mother cow stood at the other side of the pen and didn't seem interested in her baby. She sat down exhausted in the corner.

Roger said, "I was afraid this might happen." He told us that sometimes when births are difficult or there is a lot of human contact, the mother will reject her calf.

"Ohhhhhh!" moaned India as though she was really in emotional pain, the same way she says it when somebody wears a bad dress to the Oscars. Like she feels badly for them because they tried but they just didn't get it right.

Roger made the mother cow stand up and tried to get the calf to walk closer to her to nurse. Clarissa told us that the cow's milk has colostrums in it and that it's very important the calf drink right away because the colostrums has vitamins in it that will keep the calf healthy. Roger held the calf's face right next to the cow's udder. He squeezed the udder and squirted milk all over the calf's face, nose, and mouth. The calf started sucking sloppily. As the slurps got louder, Roger backed away from the cow and calf. The cow looked confused but stood there anyway.

Belly rubbed Dad's unshaven cheeks, while Clarissa and Mom leaned against the metal bars of the pen and watched the new baby. The manny pretended like he was going to give Lulu a hug with his dirty shirt, and she screamed. Dad got after her for being loud, even though it was the manny's fault.

After a little while the cow began licking the calf's back while the calf still nursed underneath her. We all cheered and clapped. Lulu and India even hugged each other and spun around in a circle together in celebration. Belly played the top of Dad's head like a snare drum.

The manny yelled, "There will be no rejection of children by their parents today!" and put his fist up in the air like he was a Jet in *West Side Story*.

Roger put his arm around the manny's shoulders and said, "Thanks for your help, Matty, I'm proud of you. You did a good job."

"Thanks, Dad," the manny said, slapping his father on his right shoulder and then keeping his hand there. He and his dad looked at each other eye to eye, like they were speaking telepathically.

"Let's name the calf Captain Fantastic," Roger suggested.

"That's one of my favorite Elton John songs," the manny said.

"I know," said the manny's dad. "Captain Fantastic it is."

Dad was standing next to me, so I wrapped a hug around his waist, and he bent down and kissed me on the top of my head.

That night I picked two postcards, both with cows on them.

Dear Uncle Max,

I helped the manny and his dad deliver a calf today. When it was done, the manny's dad told the manny that he should bring you here to visit. Then they hugged. I want to come too, because I'm kind of a natural farm kid. I can even walk bowlegged. I might want to be a vet when I grow up.

Knee-deep in afterbirth,

Keats Rufus Dalinger

Dear Sarah,

I saw a calf get born today. You would have barfed, it was so messy. The calf is named Captain Fantastic after a song. I listened to it on the manny's iPod. It's about little dirt cowboys, and the first line is "Captain Fantastic, raised and regimented, hardly a hero, just someone his mother might know."

Wish you were here,

Keats and Captain Fantastic

22 Keats Is My Favorite

The manny's mother packed a big brown paper bag full of sandwiches, fruit, and homemade cookies for us to take when we left. The sandwiches were really good because they were wrapped in waxed paper and not in plastic bags.

The adults talked by the RV while I ran up to the cow pen to say good-bye to Captain Fantastic. India went with me. Lulu was walking around the yard with Belly, who was yelling, "BYE, SKIMBLESHANKS!" "BYE ASPARAGUS!" "BYE RUM TUM TUGGER!" to all the cats.

Captain Fantastic was nursing underneath his mother. When the mother cow saw me, she walked over, and Captain Fantastic followed her. He kicked his feet in the air and jerked his head around like he was a rodeo bull. Then he ran over to me and poked his head through the fence.

"I've decided that Captain Fantastic is *your* cow." The manny's father had walked up behind me.

"Really?" I squealed. "Where will I keep him? How will I get him home? I can ride him to school!"

"Oh, we'll keep him here, but you have to come visit him. We'll keep you updated on how big he gets, and if we ever sell him, we'll send you the money for your college fund or to put toward your first car."

"Or for tickets to Dollywood!" India joked.

"I don't ever want to sell him!" I exclaimed, and rubbed Captain Fantastic on the nose. Then I ran down to the RV to tell everybody that I was a cattle rancher now.

Belly got jealous when I announced that Captain Fantastic was mine. "WELL, THE JELLICLE CATS ARE HERS, AND LOLA THE SNAKE IS HERS TOO," she said, barely keeping herself from sticking her tongue out at me.

Tears ran down Clarissa's cheeks while we said our good-byes.

"She always does this," Roger said, but his eyes got watery too as he hugged the manny and kissed him on the cheek. He said something quietly into his ear, but I couldn't hear what it was. I hope it was "Keats is my favorite." The manny smiled at his father, and then we all climbed into the RV.

Roger put his arm around Clarissa, and they looked at each other and kissed on the lips.

"Stop it! You're too old for that!" screamed Lulu. We pulled down the same long road that Cochise and the manny's father had ridden next to us on when we arrived.

Belly yelled out the window, "MEMORY, LA-LA-LOW AND THE MOONNIGHT!"

Everyone was crankier than usual as we drove through Yellowstone. Lulu had on her earbuds and refused to listen to anybody, even Mom when she asked her to help Belly rebuckle her seat belt. Mom ended up screaming it so that Lulu could hear over "(You Make Me Feel Like) A Natural Woman."

"Stop yelling," Dad scolded Mom, and put a finger in his ear like his hearing had been damaged.

"You're yelling louder than I am," Mom yelled back even louder than she had before. They sounded like Lulu and me fighting over the front seat on the way to school.

Lulu took out her earbuds and told Dad that he should stop at the next gas station to get some coffee because he and Mom were both cranky.

"I'm going to drive us into the Firehole River," Dad said, halfway joking.

"NOT THE HELLHOLE RIVER! HER DOESN'T WANT TO!" Belly squealed, and pretended to cry.

Lulu screamed, "It's called the Firehole River, Belly, and stop calling yourself 'her.' It's 'I don't want to go into the Firehole River.' Get it right. You're old enough to know."

Belly's pretend cries turned into real tears and then sobs.

"Why do you have to be so mean?" India glared at Lulu.

Mom punched Dad in the arm and glared at him for starting mass panic in the RV. The manny and I looked at each other like we were in the middle of a stampede and we didn't know which way to go.

India tried to comfort Belly and crossed over into Lulu's marked-off space.

"Get out!" Lulu screamed, and pushed India. India turned around, grabbed the conduct mark board, and ripped it in half.

"This is anarchy!" screamed Lulu. "This is why we have these rules!"

"Okay! Enough!" erupted the manny like Old Faithful. I'd been waiting to use an Old Faithful analogy since we visited it earlier that morning. The RV got silent. We had never really heard the manny yell, unless you count the time he stepped on one of my LEGOs and dropped a tray of oysters on the floor. He served us oysters once for an after-school snack just to mix it up. But that was a yell of pain. This was different. And oysters are gross.

Dad pulled into a scenic overlook next to the road and walked into the back of the RV. Then the yelling started up again with Lulu. "I'm so tired of being trapped in here with all these babies!"

India rolled her eyes at her.

"I'm almost in high school, and I shouldn't have to spend my whole summer with little kids. I need to have some adult time!" Lulu went on.

I said, "You mean like with Fletcher when you kissed!"

"How do you know about that?" Lulu whirled toward me.

I shrugged, even though I had overheard Lulu talking about it to Margo on the bus.

"OOOOOOOH," said Belly like they do on television shows when teenagers kiss.

"What?" Mom chimed in.

"Nothing, Mommy," said Lulu, putting on her sweet-child voice and look, the same ones she does when she wants to order a new shirt online from Urban Outfitters. She always says, "Mommy? Can I order a shirt? It's really pretty." She never calls Mom "Mommy" unless she wants to order something. Mom always falls for it.

"Did you give him the tongue?" I asked, not really knowing what "giving the tongue" meant.

"Keats!" Mom slapped my leg with her hand. "Don't talk like that ever!"

"Well, excuuuuuse me!" I said snottily. We've all picked up a little bit from Lulu.

Dad said, "Look, this is a vacation! Can we please try to have some fun and get along?"

"I'm having fun, Dad," I said, taking the opportunity to show him that I'm his best child. I really wasn't having much fun. Mom was glaring at me because of my tongue comment, and I could tell that it would be awhile before she would forget about it.

"I'm not!" shouted Lulu so loudly that Dad shushed her and glanced out the window to notice that a family in a brand-new white Mercedes station wagon had pulled up next to us. Lulu looked to see what Dad was looking at. They looked like the perfect family. Perfect haircuts. Perfect teeth. Perfect collars popped up on their golf shirts. I popped up my collar too.

The station wagon had a mom and a dad in the front seats and three kids about the same ages as Lulu, India, and me in the backseat. The window was cracked about half an inch, and the dad was yelling something at the mom about not being able to read a map. She was yelling back at him and called him stupid. The girl Lulu's age saw Lulu and rolled her eyes and shook her head toward her parents. The kids in the car looked miserable and weren't even talking to one another.

"If that dad were riding in here, he'd already have three conduct marks," said Lulu.

Mom laughed and so did Belly, even though she didn't know what was funny. Dad settled back into the driver's seat and we stopped arguing.

The manny looked at the girl Lulu's age in the station wagon. He put his pointer finger under his chin and lifted his head with it. It means "Keep your chin up." The manny made the same motion to Belly one time during a Bible school program. Belly goes to Bible school with her friend Adam. Belly had one line in the program at the end of the week: "God loves cheerful givers!" She practiced it all week, but during the program she stood up and yelled into the microphone, "GOD LOVES CHICKEN LIVERS!" The audience started laughing really loudly, and Belly's face got red and she looked like she was going to cry. That's when the manny made the "Keep your chin up" sign.

After the program the manny told Belly, "God probably does love chicken livers."

"And chicken nuggets," Belly added.

The girl in the station wagon smiled, waved a forced wave to us, put on a pair of sunglasses, and sank lower into her seat.

Dear Uncle Max,

Yellowstone is the world's first national park. I used Mom's camera to take a picture of Belly feeding gummy bears to a ground squirrel. I also used it to get a picture of Dad getting a lecture from a park ranger about feeding the wildlife. You'll see it when I give my PowerPoint slide show when I get home.

I think I want to be a park ranger when I grow up.

Keats Rufus Dalinger

Dear Sarah,

Does your family fight on vacation?

Just wondering,

Keats

The hotel in Salt Lake City was called the Little America. It was a weird burgundy color and had a big courtyard with a swimming pool in the middle of it. The lounge chairs at the pool had crisp white towels rolled up on them, and there was a stereo system that was playing "Young at Heart" by Frank Sinatra.

Frank Sinatra music wasn't playing in the lobby. Instead a man in a tuxedo was playing a big, shiny black piano next to five big couches. There was a chandelier hanging from the ceiling, and all the countertops were white marble.

"I feel like I've traveled back in time," said India.

"Do I look younger?" asked the manny.

"No. You still look thirty-four, but you look like a thirty-four-year-old at a nineteen fifties hotel," India said before she jumped out of the way of a gold luggage cart that was being pushed by a blond bellhop in an all-white uniform and hat. The hat had a strap that went around his chin, and his name tag said CHIP.

Mom stared at him, and Dad caught her. She claimed that she was admiring his perfect skin. "He doesn't look like he's ever had a piece of chocolate in his life," she said. Chocolate makes Mom's face break out in pimples like a teenager's. So do periods.

Our hotel room was on the top floor and had a balcony that overlooked the city. Mom pointed out the Mormon Temple and the capitol building. The temple looked like a white castle with sharp points at the top.

Lulu read parts of *To Kill a Mockingbird* out loud while Belly looked down at the city and pointed things out. A trolley car. A "Got Milk?" billboard. Bird poop on the windshields of cars below. She kept scanning the city until she found something to point out.

"PARADE!" shouted Belly as she jumped up and down and pointed down to a street a couple of blocks away. There was a line of floats and marching bands along the street. Then she ran to the bathroom, screaming and holding herself because her excitement was too much to hold in. Belly loves parades. They make her pee.

Belly ran back out to the balcony before her pants were even all the way up. "CAN HER GO?

THEY'RE THROWING SUGAR! HER NEEDS SUGAR!" she screamed as she straightened her Hello Kitty panties, which were twisted around her waist and looked uncomfortable. Belly calls all candy sugar.

"I need sugar too!" the manny screamed, even though it was obvious that he didn't.

"Let's go see what the parade is for," Mom said.

The manny and Belly gave each other a high five, and then the manny held on to his palm like Belly had slapped him too hard. She giggled.

We raced through the hotel lobby and past the piano player, who was taking a break outside the carousel doors. He looked like a mobster in his tuxedo, glancing at his watch and smoking a cigarette. I told India that he probably played the piano during the daytime and threw people with cement blocks on their feet into the Great Salt Lake at night. India laughed but couldn't say anything back because Belly had ahold of her hand and was pulling her down the street toward the parade.

The parade hadn't started yet, but people were lining up, getting ready for it to begin. There were police all around, on horses and motorcycles. Mom told Belly that the police were there to make sure that kids didn't take more than their fair share of candy that was thrown off of the parade floats. Belly looked scared. The only thing that keeps her from causing trouble is the threat of jail.

We stood at the very beginning of the parade, where the organizer was telling which float, band, or group to go next through a megaphone. The first to go were a bunch of women in jeans and black leather boots on motorcycles. Belly held her ears as the bikes roared away. I could feel the noise inside my chest. The same way I can feel fireworks shows in my toes. The crowd cheered. So did the people waiting for their turn to go. After the bikes went, thirty men in Speedo swimsuits holding volleyballs started walking behind a sign that said SALT LAKE CITY WATER POLO. One of them carried a stereo that was playing a David Bowie song that Lulu has on her iPod. The one that goes, "Take a look at the Lawman beating up the wrong guy," and where "Mickey Mouse has grown up a cow." It's a weird song. Lulu sang along, but she covered her eyes with her hands. She hates Speedo swimsuits. I've never seen a water polo team in a parade before, especially in their swimsuits. India said that it was a "flock of *Glamour* Don'ts."

"Aha," said the manny like he had figured out

what the celebration was about. Mom squeezed his arm like she was in on his discovery.

Belly ran all over the street, grabbing candy that was thrown from floats. A man who was running for sheriff threw Jolly Ranchers from on top of a horse. A Delta Airlines float shaped like an airplane threw out Delta Airlines necklaces. The Salt Lake Men's Choir sang, "'R-E-S-P-E-C-T,'" and threw out chewing gum. Belly picked up three pieces but then handed two of them to smaller kids when she spotted a policeman standing on the corner. She waved to the policeman and pretended that she was helping other kids get candy.

The next float standing in line to go had a big sign that said PFLAG. I'm not sure how you say it, but I think the *P* is silent, like in the word "psychic." The lady at the front of the float had a microphone. She pointed at the manny and said, "Hey, cute guy with the sunhat, do you want to ride on our float?"

The manny looked around and then dramatically pointed to himself and mouthed, "Me?" like they do in the movies when they're crowned homecoming queen. Then he yelled, "Only because you said I was cute," and started to climb up on the float.

That's the thing about the manny. He gets

asked to join in on things. Mom says it's because the manny could have fun inside a paper bag.

"I'll see you at the end of the parade!" the manny yelled down to us. I turned around and saw Mom and Dad laughing.

"I'm going with him!" I yelled, wanting people to think I could have fun in a paper bag too. And I didn't want to miss anything. Like if the manny started lip-synching to "Twist and Shout" like they do in the parade in *Ferris Bueller's Day Off*.

Before Mom and Dad could object, I ran toward the float and leaped up and pulled myself on beside the manny. I turned around and waved at Mom and Dad. Lulu and India didn't notice. They were trying to get Belly to spit out the seven pieces of gum she had shoved in her mouth. The wad was so big that when Belly finally spit it out, it looked like she'd spit out her pink chewed-up brain. A policeman stepped on it.

The float whizzed around the corner, and I started waving to people along the street. The manny stood behind me with his hands on my shoulders, making sure that I didn't fall or lose my balance. The parade went right by the Mormon Temple. It's even prettier up close, like an ice princess's house.

We went by an apartment building that had

balconies. There was a group of older women out there hollering and waving down at the water polo team. One of them even screamed, "We love you," as she danced to a Beyoncé song that was now playing.

Some of the polo players yelled back, "We love you, too!"

There was a man on the float with us named Tony. He wore big wire-rimmed glasses with tinted lenses and told the manny that he was a retired airport employee.

Tony shook the manny's hand and said, "I'm here for my son. He was just named Elementary School Teacher of the Year in his school district in Seattle."

"Wow, that's great," said the manny. "You must be very proud."

"Yes. He's going to change the world . . . at least a little bit." Then Tony threw a handful of peppermint candy out to a group of people sitting in lawn chairs on the street curb.

Next to the people in the lawn chairs was a group of people holding black signs with white writing on them and yelling things at the people in the parade.

"YOU'RE DISGUSTING!" yelled a woman in a long dress, holding a sign that said NOT HERE! THIS IS GOD'S LAND!

Another man held a sign that said GOD HATES WHAT YOU DO!

Tony and some others yelled back, but not meanly. They yelled, "Peace and understanding! Have a good day!" and kept waving and smiling.

"FAGGOTS!" the man yelled back.

I had heard that word before and knew that it was hateful, even more hateful than "queer." I looked up at the manny's eyes to see if he had heard. He looked like he couldn't breathe or like he might throw up. Like if he exhaled, his tear dam would break. That's what India calls it when welled-up eyes turn into flowing streams of tears. It happened to her at Grandma's funeral when Uncle Max told the story about how Grandma had told him he was "opening up her whole life" when he told her he was gay.

Tony must have noticed the manny's eyes too.

"Don't let them get to you," he said. "They don't understand how hateful they sound. They haven't educated themselves yet." The manny smiled and nodded, but his eyes were watery. Then my eyes got watery. I turned around and hugged the manny around his waist, pressing my head against his stomach. He hugged me back around my head. Then the manny let go of me and started waving and smiling to the people holding the signs.

I reached into the bucket of peppermint candy and threw a handful on the ground in front of the picketers. I thought about throwing them really hard right at their heads, but I didn't. The woman in the long dress bent down, picked one up, and unwrapped it. She looked up at me as she put it in her mouth.

I smiled at her and waved and wondered how uncomfortable her skin must be to walk around in that it would make her so mean.

I took the postcard that I was going to send to Uncle Max and wrote one to the manny and put it on his pillow that night while he was in the bathroom brushing his teeth.

Dear Manny,

I think you are very brave.

I love you.

Keats

24 Barf du Soleil

Before we left Salt Lake City, we swam in the swimming pool at Little America one last time so Belly wouldn't throw a tantrum, or as I heard Mom say, so Belly would "get tired and sleep most of the way to Las Vegas." Lulu didn't swim. She sat on the side with her legs in the pool and read a *USA Today* article about Katie Couric, the news anchor. Katie Couric is one of Lulu's heroes. I read it in the hero list in her diary. She was right under Eleanor Roosevelt and right above Amelia Earhart.

Mom and Dad had taken us to eat breakfast in the cafeteria, but we ate really fast so that we could get one more swim in. The manny shoved two pieces of sausage in his mouth, storing some in his cheeks while he chewed. Mom told him to slow down and set a good example after Belly started eating right off the plate without a fork so she could finish fast. I love it when the manny gets in trouble from Mom. He pushes his bottom lip out and pouts.

Mom almost didn't let Belly come swim with us because she gargled her orange juice at the table the way Dad does with mouthwash every morning. I kind of hoped Mom wouldn't let Belly come swimming, because she screams and does cannonballs the whole time and drives away the other families. Mom did let her. I think Mom probably needed a break from Belly. We all need breaks from her sometimes. India says that Belly is "cute, but she is always up in your grill." Your grill is your face.

India practiced her water ballet by pointing her toes and straight legs out of the water. She kicked them and then went underwater and came up with her fluttering hands. She started doing it after she saw her friends doing synchronized swimming at the Golf and Tennis swimming pool. I can't remember the friends' first names. Everybody just calls them the Binger sisters, and they always wear matching swimsuits and go everywhere together, even to the bathroom. They synchronize *everything*. India must think that the Binger sisters are a *Glamour* Do, because she's always copying them.

While India held on to the edge of the pool and practiced her toe point in the air, the manny stood in the pool and judged Belly's and my splashes from cannonballs and screwdrivers. My splashes were bigger, but every once in a while the manny would tell Belly that she had won, and then he'd wink at me so I'd know he was just making her feel good. He even pretended to drown from one of Belly's splashes.

"You nearly killed me!" he screeched, coughing, spitting water, and flailing around.

One of Belly's splashes *was* big. So big that it splashed Lulu and her *USA Today* newspaper that she was reading.

"You got Katie Couric all wet," she said, pointing to the picture that had a big, wet splotch right under Katie Couric's chin, which made it look like a beard.

"Gosh, she really looks like Matt Lauer with that beard," the manny joked. Matt Lauer used to be Katie Couric's cohost on the *Today* show. He's the one that Tom Cruise called "glib" on television. I think "glib" must mean "tall and handsome."

Lulu didn't think the manny was funny. She pulled her feet out of the water and walked over to a chair that was far enough away that Belly couldn't splash liver spots all over Katie's face. Or at least that's what the manny said.

Belly was OC at the pool. That's what the manny calls "out of control." She wouldn't just swim around nicely. She kept screaming,

"WATCH THIS!" and she'd do a belly flop; or, "TEACHER'S SEAT!" and she'd jump in with her legs crossed and her back straight, like she thought teachers sit. She even mooned India when India told her that she was being inconsiderate to the other swimmers.

There weren't many other swimmers. Just a dad with a hairy chest teaching his baby how to swim. The baby was just giggling and laughing when the dad would take him under the water. Then, when he came up, he'd scream with excitement and look like his eyes were going to pop out of his head. They kept moving to other spots in the swimming pool because Belly would get closer and closer to them, trying to splash the baby to make him laugh.

Mom and Dad walked over to the pool after they had finished breakfast.

"WATCH THIS!" Belly screamed so loudly that the entire pool area looked over at her.

She ran as fast as she could toward the pool. When she got to the edge of the pool, she got a look of terror on her face. Belly's toes left the concrete right as she opened her mouth and threw up into the swimming pool. It landed in the water, and then *she* landed in the water . . . right on top of her own throw-up. Little bits of eggs Benedict and toast and bright orange liquid flew into the air. Some floated on the top of the pool. The dad and his baby quickly walked up the steps and started to dry off.

I swam to the edge and pulled myself out of the pool before Belly even came up for air. The manny ran through the water to grab Belly and pull her out. When Belly came up from underneath the water, she was already sobbing and her face was bright red.

"AAAAAHHHHHHHH!" she wailed so loudly that the swimming baby started to cry too. The dad wrapped him in a fluffy white towel, and they hurried to their hotel room.

"Come here, sweetie," Mom said, taking Belly into a towel too and holding her the way you rock a baby. Belly kept wailing. I kept trying not to look at the barf floating on top of the swimming pool. I tried not to look at the barf on the manny's chest. Lulu wasn't looking. She had the Katie Couric article covering her face. She says she has a weak stomach and can't stand to see or hear other people throw up. She once spent a school day in the principal's office organizing his personal library because a boy threw up in her classroom and the janitor came and put that pink powder on it and let it sit for a while. Even after it was all cleaned up, she refused to go back to the classroom.

Instead she sat at the principal's big oak desk and helped him answer e-mails from concerned parents about dress codes and the school lunch program.

The hotel management didn't sprinkle pink powder on Belly's throw up in the pool. Instead they told Mom that they would have to drain the pool and fill it back up with new water.

"I'm so sorry," Mom apologized.

"Don't worry about it," said the hotel manager. "It happens all the time."

"Ewwww!" India and I said at the same time, and looked at each other.

Belly was still crying when we got into the RV to drive toward Las Vegas. Lulu tried to make her feel better by saying, "That article about Katie Couric sure was interesting. Did you know that *she* threw up in a swimming pool a few summers ago while they were filming a special wedding segment for the *Today* show?"

Belly stopped crying. "Really?" she said, even though she probably didn't know who Katie Couric was.

"Yep," said Lulu. "She just cleaned herself off and moved on with her life. Barf happens." Then she shrugged.

The manny giggled with his shoulders when Lulu said "Barf happens."

Belly dried off her tears with her hands and tried to move on with her life.

I grabbed the paper and scanned the article but didn't see anything about Katie Couric barfing in a swimming pool. When I looked at Lulu, she rolled her eyes at me. I guess Lulu was just being kind.

Dear Uncle Max,

VEGAS HERE WE COME! Dad won't stop doing his Elvis impressions. Belly keeps copying him. She's better than he is. I heard Lulu talking to you on the telephone. Why were you talking to her? I'm not being nosy. I'm just practicing my journalism skills like Katie Couric.

When happy in Vegas, stay in Vegas,

Keats Rufus Dalinger

Dear Sarah,

You're never going to believe what happened. Belly projectile vomited into the hotel swimming pool while she was in midair, and then she landed in it. The manny called it "Barf du Soleil," but not in front of Belly because she's embarrassed about it. India says that we left "the mark of the Dalingers" on Salt Lake City, but I don't know what she means by that.

Do you think we could sell Belly on eBay? Opening bid: 30 cents.

I'll write you from Las Vegas,

Keats

25 Nobody Puts Baby in a Corner

Glass flowers hang from the ceiling of the hotel Bellagio in Las Vegas. It's a sculpture by a guy named Chihuly. India counted the different colors while Mom and Dad checked into the hotel. Lulu kept rereading parts of *To Kill a Mockingbird*. Belly was staring at a lady in a wheelchair who reminded me of Grandma before she died. She smelled like Estee Lauder and had silver bracelets and necklaces on that matched her shiny wheelchair. She must have reminded Belly of Grandma too, because Belly grabbed ahold of the lady's hand while I asked her questions. "What is your favorite color?" "What is your favorite five o'clock cocktail?" I used to carry Grandma's five o'clock cocktail out to her every evening when Grandma lived in the hospital bed in our living room before she died.

The lady in the wheelchair answered, "Light blue," and, "Gin and tonic on the rocks with a squeeze of lime." Just like Grandma.

Belly climbed up in her lap and asked for a ride around the lobby.

"Belly, no!" scolded Lulu, holding her place in *To Kill a Mockingbird* with her finger. "I'm sorry," she apologized.

"Don't be," the lady in the wheelchair said. "You keep reading your book. I'll entertain this pretty young lady."

"I'm pretty," Belly said, nodding her head and agreeing with the lady in the wheelchair. She didn't say it in her foghorn voice, and she didn't call herself "her." She used a really calm voice like she had good manners and was polite. The lady probably had no idea that at any minute Belly might ask her to pull her finger, like she did to Dad's boss at last year's office Christmas party. Dad's boss joked that maybe Dad could use his bonus to send Belly off to finishing school.

The lady started rolling her wheelchair through the lobby, while Belly raised her hands in the air and said, "Whee!" like she was on a roller coaster ride. The lady looked like she was on a ride too. Her cheeks were red and she had a big smile on her face.

The manny followed them, probably to make sure Belly didn't steal the lady's purse or steer the wheelchair into a fountain. She didn't. She just rode nicely like a normal little girl. I've never seen her act like a person before. She usually acts like a wild animal or a dog from the pound. Belly even kissed the lady in the wheelchair on the cheek and thanked her for the ride before she climbed down, grabbed Mom's hand, and walked with us to the elevators.

Belly returned to being a wild animal again when we got to the floor that our hotel room was on. She jumped out of the elevator, screamed, and ran down the long hallway and tried to do cartwheels. They looked more like donkey kicks, though, because her legs didn't go over her head. They just went sideways into the air, and then she'd say, "TAA-DAA!"

"Shhhhh!" Mom told her, but it was too late. The door across from where we were entering our room opened up a crack and somebody yelled, "Quiet down, you pesky kids!" in a really mean voice.

"OOOOOOO! GRUMPY!" Belly said, the same way the manny does to her when she's grumpy. The manny covered up Belly's mouth gently with his hand.

"We're very sorry, sir . . . ," the manny started to apologize to the partially cracked door. Just then the door opened up all the way and Uncle Max was standing there. Uncle Max was here! The manny leaped at him and squeezed a hug around his neck, the same way I do to Mom and Dad when they come back from a long trip.

"IT'S UNCLE MAX THAT'S THE GRUMPY OLD MAN!" yelled Belly.

"Usually," said the manny, joking. I started jumping up and down and gave Uncle Max a hug too. So did India. Lulu, Mom, and Dad did too, but it was strange—they didn't act nearly as surprised to see him.

We started asking Uncle Max all kinds of questions.

"What are you doing here?"

"How are the paintings going?"

"Why does the manny call you Sugar Bear?"

We went into Uncle Max's room and collapsed on his bed and in the chairs. There was a bouquet of flowers and a card on the table by the bed. They were dark burgundy calla lilies, the manny's favorite. The manny opened up the envelope, read the card, and smiled really big. He gave Uncle Max another hug and whispered something to him. I didn't even try to hear what it was because it wasn't my business, but I bet it was, "Nobody puts Baby in a corner." The manny's always saying that. It's his favorite line from *Dirty Dancing*.

Dear Sarah,

Uncle Max is here! The manny is so happy! And I am too.

The manny says that when he dies, he wants his ashes spread over the fountains of the Bellagio while they play the song "Time to Say Goodbye" by Andrea Bocelli. Uncle Max said that he wants his whole body dropped from a helicopter into the fountains during the finale of "Hey, Big Spender." Mom told them that she's probably just going to flush them both down the toilet when they die, like we did India's goldfish, John. The manny says it's ironic that his name was John and he got flushed down the john.

Vegas, baby!

Keats

Lulu, India, and I are sharing a hotel room, and Belly is sharing with Mom and Dad. Our hotel rooms join together with a door. Lulu wants to keep it closed, but Mom and Dad are making her keep it open to make sure that we don't order room-service chocolate malts or rent an R-rated movie off the television. I've seen only one R-rated movie. It was called *Billy Elliot*, and Mom rented it for us one night. She had seen it in the theater and thought it had a good message. It's about a little boy who wants to go to the Royal Ballet School to become a dancer even though his father doesn't think boys should do ballet. His father changes his mind at the end and is proud when Billy is the star of an all-male version of the ballet *Swan Lake*. Mom cried at the end. She also cried at the end of *Finding Nemo* when Nemo and his father see each other again.

The manny is sharing the room with Uncle Max across the hall. They slept late this morning because they went out to a late dinner last night. India said that they are probably tired because they drank too much wine. I put a chair up next to our door so that I could stand on it to see through the little eyehole. Whenever I heard a noise or movement in the hallway, I ran over to see if it was the manny and Uncle Max. I saw the housekeeper. I saw room service. I saw a dressed-up woman with fancy jewelry pick her nose. She must have forgotten that people can see her through the peepholes in their doors.

When they did finally come out of their room, Uncle Max was wearing a crisp white shirt and jeans, and the manny was wearing a black Lacoste golf shirt and khaki pants with a striped belt. I saw what they were wearing and ran to the closet to change. I was definitely underdressed for what we were going to do today. Maybe we were going to have lunch at Siegfried and Roy's mansion. I bet the manny knows them. I had on an "I ♥ NY" T-shirt that Dad had brought me from a business trip, but I changed into my black Lacoste golf shirt. Mine isn't really Lacoste, but it is black. Lulu called me Mini-Me for the rest of the day, but the manny said that "imitation is the sincerest form of flattery." He told me that the clothing designer Zac Posen is always imitating his style for his fashion line and that's why "young Hollywood looks so put together these days." India said that if Zac Posen really imitated the manny's style, there would be a lot more women with shaved heads, leather loafers, and patches of hair on their chins that they missed while shaving, a definite *Glamour* Don't. She said Zac Posen is always a *Glamour* Do, even when he wears a metallic gold sport coat.

We didn't go have lunch at Siegfried and Roy's mansion. We went shopping at a place called Caesars Palace. In the middle of the shops there are statues of Roman gods that talk and move. A big crowd gathered, and we watched the King Atlas statue decide which of his children would rule Atlantis next. They fought over it until King Atlas started yelling and the walls began to thunder. Belly had to get up on Dad's shoulders because she was scared. I didn't really pay attention to the show because there was a brown velvet blazer in the window of Banana Republic that I kept staring at. It looked like cake frosting.

Caesars Palace is also where Elton John has his concert when Céline Dion isn't using the stage. Dad bought us all tickets to the 7:30 show and said it was his gift to Uncle Max and the manny. They must be celebrating something special, because Dad doesn't usually give gifts. He usually lets Mom take care of that and just signs the cards where Mom points. Maybe Uncle Max and the manny were celebrating Uncle Max's painting show. Or maybe it was Oprah's birthday again. The manny always celebrates that.

Belly got tired and cranky, so we went back to the Bellagio so she could take a nap in the hotel room. When Belly gets tired and cranky, she throws herself on the floor and does her frustrated cry, with lots of yelling sobs but no real tears. Mom is usually good at knowing when Belly is about to get tired and cranky, but this one sneaked up on us in the middle of Gap Kids. Before Mom could grab Belly and bribe her with candy from her purse or a chocolate chip cookie from Mrs. Fields, Belly threw herself onto the floor. She rolled underneath a table of striped baby sweaters, fake-sobbing and kicking the table leg. A pregnant lady was holding up one of the sweaters and showing her husband. Dad said it must be their first child, because nobody shops for their babies the second or third time around. The pregnant lady got a worried look on her face and started to cry. Her husband tried to comfort her by putting his arm around her. He made eye contact with Mom and said, "She's just really emotional these days."

Mom smiled and said, "It's not always like this. Sometimes she knocks over the window display."

The pregnant lady laughed through her tears

while Mom grabbed Belly and said, "Let's go back to the room so you can embarrass me in private."

"We all need to rest anyway," Uncle Max added. "We have a big night tonight."

We're going to the Elton John concert and then to a surprise that Uncle Max planned. Lulu's trying to figure out what the surprise is because she doesn't want to be tricked into going someplace that has topless showgirls. She says that topless showgirls make her uncomfortable. I'm not sure how she knows.

Dear Sarah,

Uncle Max has a surprise for us tonight after the Elton John concert. I think it might be meeting Elton John. If it is, I'll get you an autographed copy of the *Lion King* sound track. I'm going to bow and say, "The pleasure is mine, Sir Elton John," since he was made a knight by Queen Elizabeth. I hope I don't throw up on him with excitement. His outfits look like they would be expensive to dry-clean. I think Lulu knows what the surprise is, but she won't tell me.

Maybe it's written in her diary. I gotta go.

Keats

27 The Itch Is Back

Mom wore fancy gray slacks and a silky cream shirt that flowed like a flag in the wind when she walked. Her high heels made her as tall as Dad and Uncle Max, and taller than the manny. She looked like a model in a fashion show and even walked differently, like she couldn't keep up with her legs. Instead of her usual gigantic purse she carried a small, jeweled bag that had only Kleenex and Altoids inside. Belly would probably ask for both during the Elton John concert.

Lulu, India, and Belly all had fancy dresses on too. Belly wore hers with a pair of purple rain boots with daisies painted on the sides. Mom didn't make her change into her nice shoes because she likes to let Belly express herself. We don't know what it is that Belly's trying to express, but one time she wore toilet paper around the top of her head like a turban to a birthday party.

Dad looked like he does when he goes to work:

blue suit, white shirt, and tie. He wore the orange pocket square in his front jacket pocket for a "splash of color." That's what I wrote on the Father's Day card when I gave him the pocket square. Dad asked me to fluff it just right and stuff it in his pocket because I have the touch.

Uncle Max thinks I have the touch too. He asked my opinion on his shoes. I chose black pointy leather oxfords. He wore them with a black suit. The manny wore black too, except he wore a white shirt, suspenders, and a floppy black bow tie from last fall's Barneys CO-OP catalog. I wanted to wear suspenders too, but I was worried that Lulu would call me Mini-Me again. And I didn't have suspenders. India gave us each her *Glamour* Do approval as she held the hotel room door for us to go through. She made Dad go back into the bathroom and put more product in his hair. Then she gave him a faux-hawk.

Instead of suspenders I wore slacks, a starched white shirt, and a green sweater vest. I saw the same look in the window of the Brooks Brothers store at the Forum Shops at Caesars Palace. As we were walking through the hotel lobby on the way to the concert, the manny even said, "You look just like the window display at Brooks Brothers."

"I *do*?" I asked, scrunching up my face and pretending that I didn't know that I looked like the window display.

The manny just nodded. I put my hands in my pockets and walked the way businessmen do on Saturdays, like I was happy to be going to a football game or a pumpkin sale instead of sitting in front of a computer typing in quarterly reports. Dad does quarterly reports. It's when you report on how many quarters you have in the bank.

Our seats at the Elton John concert were right in the middle of the first floor. We could see the stage perfectly without binoculars or standing on the chairs. There was a big red piano on the left side of the stage and neon signs that said ELTON on the right side. Everybody was dressed really fancy and carried martini glasses with olives or glasses of wine. I felt like I was at the opera. I've never been to the opera, but I bet people dress up and carry cocktails.

As soon as the concert started, I knew I wasn't at the opera. Elton John came out onstage, and the whole audience screamed and stood up. A lady in a red strapless dress screamed, "YOU ROCK!" I don't think that happens at the opera. I also don't think that they would have blow-up fruit and big blow-up boobs on the stage at the opera.

Elton John wore a bright red suit that India called Nehru. She announced to herself loud enough for all of us to hear, "He is such a *Glamour* Don't that he's a *Glamour* Do." Then she sighed like she was in love.

"I was hoping he'd play more of his *Lion King* songs," Lulu said, leaning over to India. "Céline would never sing this song." Elton John was singing a wild song that had the *B* word in it, while a big video of Pamela Anderson swinging around a pole played behind him. Lulu had her hands over her eyes. She hates pole dancing and she hates the *B* word. I don't really like it either, but I read in *People* magazine that women in the suburbs are taking pole-dancing classes for exercise. I told Mom that she should get a pole for our garage, to go with our weight bench and Thighmaster. India was moving her knees up and down to the same beat that Pamela Anderson was swinging around the pole.

Mom, Dad, Uncle Max, and the manny sang to nearly every song. "Philadelphia Freedom." "Your Song." "Levon." Mom even put her hands up in the air and waved them around while she sang along with "Rocket Man." Lulu calmly asked her to please stop because security was looking at her.

When Elton John was introducing one song, he said, "This one goes out to all the sugar bears out there." I looked over and saw Uncle Max squeeze the manny's knee with his hand. The manny's hand was on top of Uncle Max's hand. He had his eyes closed and he started mouthing the words. The manny put his arm around Uncle Max when it got to a part that said "And someone saved my life tonight sugar bear." At the end of the song I leaned over to Uncle Max and said, "You're a free butterfly, Sugar Bear." He winked at me.

Belly was asleep by the time the concert was over. She even slept through the standing ovation and Elton John yelling, "Thank you! I love you!" in his British accent. Belly had six Altoids lined up and pressed into her bare leg, and Kleenexes stuffed into her ears. Her purple rain boots were on the floor, and her bare feet were sprawled across Mom's nice clothes. Mom still looked like she was a fashion model, but not for *Vogue*. More like *Ladies' Home Journal*.

The lights came up in the theater, and the manny and Uncle Max looked energized, like they had just woken up from a nap. Their faces were beaming like Belly's does on Christmas morning when she runs into the room and jumps on the pile of presents.

Dad stood up and picked up Belly, who woke up and scrambled to save the Altoids that were falling to the floor.

"Céline will get them," said the manny. "She loves Altoids. She eats them for dinner."

Lulu punched the manny in the arm.

On the way out of the theater we talked about our favorite parts of the concert.

"I liked the big blow-up boobs!" Dad said, laughing.

"I liked 'Tiny Dancer,'" Mom said.

"My favorite song was 'Daniel,'" said India.

Belly made Dad put her down so she could show us her favorite part. "I LIKED THE ITCH, THE ITCH, THE ITCH IS BACK." Belly started jumping up and down like crazy and pretended to be scratching itches all over her body. She looked like she was being attacked by ants.

The song didn't really say "The itch is back." It said something else, but nobody corrected Belly.

"What about 'Circle of Life'?" Mom asked.

"NO, THE ITCH SONG!" Belly said, letting out a big breath and lowering her shoulders like she was completely happy.

Lulu changed the subject. "My favorite part was when Elton made eye contact with me and said, 'Thank you. I love you.'" She called him

Elton just like she calls Céline Dion, Céline. Like they went to college together.

"GOY!" Mom said, and then high-fived me like she was in my class and we were out at recess.

I sang "You're a butterfly. And butterflies are free to fly" in my mind while we walked to wherever Uncle Max was taking us. I couldn't wait. Maybe it was side-by-side massages. I've never had a massage.

Someone Saved My Life Tonight,
Sugar Bear

We walked down the Strip, still excited from the concert. The Strip is the main road in Las Vegas, where all the casinos are lined up: New York–New York. Paris Las Vegas. Treasure Island.

India wouldn't stop chattering. She said she was going to try to re-create a couple of Elton John's outfits for the manny.

"I don't know," said the manny. "You have to be pretty confident to wear some of those things."

"You're confident!" India said back. "Remember when you wore your bathrobe to Lulu's spa birthday party?" Lulu had a spa birthday party for her last birthday. Her friends came over to the house, and Lulu hired India to give them all pedicures and manicures. She hired me to give them all shoulder rubs. They even went into the bathroom, turned on the hot water in the shower, and pretended that they were in a steam room. The manny wore his robe and served glasses of

water with cucumber slices in them, and straw-
berries and whipped cream.

"I remember," said Lulu. "I had to send notes
of apology instead of thank-you notes to all my
friends." Lulu is starting to pick up on the manny's humor.

Uncle Max laughed at Lulu's joke and squeezed
the manny's shoulder like they do in the movies
when they say "No hard feelings."

Uncle Max kept his hand on the manny's
shoulder until we got back to the Bellagio.

"I thought you had a surprise for us," I pro-
tested as we walked under the Chihuly sculp-
tured ceiling.

"We're *going*!" Uncle Max said to me like he
was my age and we were fighting in the car. He
said it really snotty like Lulu does. "Hold your
horses! Keep your pants on!" he kept saying.

He led us to the botanical garden, which has
a big tree that is 120 years old. The tree was
surrounded by rosebushes, daisies, and other
colorful flowers, which Belly kept trying to pick.
Mom got after her, but she sparkled her eyes.
Belly can sparkle her eyes and smile and be really
cute when she wants to. Mom calls it her sweet
look. I practiced a sweet look in the mirror, but
it looked forced. It looked more like I had bad
gas or a bladder problem. Belly's looks natural.

Belly kept her sweet look on the whole time we were in the botanical garden. When we got to the base of the big tree, there was a man standing there with a white suit on and sparkly, big glasses. He looked just like Elton John. I thought it was Elton John at first, but when he spoke, he didn't have a British accent. He sounded more like the cabdriver from my trip with Grandma to New York City. The cabdriver called Grandma "sweet cheeks," so she tipped him a dollar extra.

The Elton John look-alike said, "Yo. You Max?" There was a small woman with a portable CD player standing next to him.

Uncle Max smiled and nodded. How did they know each other? Was our surprise going to be that Uncle Max had joined the mob and we all had to move to Italy and join the witness pro-tection program? I'd dye my hair black and change my name to Rico and drink red wine from a bottle in a paper bag. I think you can drink wine when you're ten in Italy. Nobody would ever know that it was me, because the real me would never have black hair or drink wine. Especially from a paper bag.

"This is Matthew," Uncle Max introduced the manny to mafia Elton John, who had a small book in his hand and a rope hanging around his neck. He looked like he had just graduated from the School of Crocodile Rock. That's what India whispered to me.

"Pleasure," mafia Elton John said in his *Sopranos* voice. I've never seen *The Sopranos*, but Craig watches it and is always saying things like "I got issues!" and "Who got whacked?" when we're out on the playground.

Uncle Max turned to us and said, "This is the surprise." Mom squealed and hugged Uncle Max and then Matthew. Dad shook both of their hands. I had no idea what was going on. *This* was our surprise? I was kind of hoping for a helicopter ride over the Hoover Dam or show-girl dance lessons. Lulu pulled her *To Kill a Mockingbird* book out of her pocket and flipped through it like she was preparing to read something. India asked Lulu something quietly in her ear. Lulu leaned in to India and quietly said something back. I think they were planning their escape from the witness protection program.

"Ohhhh!" India said like she'd just solved a mystery. In the cartoons there would have been a lightbulb over her head. Belly didn't have any idea what was going on. She was still concentrating on her sweet look. She was starting to look like a mannequin or like those creepy kids in the horror movies who never blink.

Uncle Max and the manny stood in front of mafia Elton John, who said in an official voice, "We are gathered here today to celebrate the love between Matthew and Maximilian." Mom squeezed Dad's hand. I grabbed on to Belly's and squeezed it. It made her blink. Finally.

This was our surprise! I stared up at Uncle Max's and the manny's faces. They looked really happy. Their smiles were so big that you could see their gums. The Elton John look-alike kept talking about how the world needs more love in it, and about how when people love each other, it can be contagious and passed on to other people, making the world happier. He said it better than that. I don't think he used the word "contagious." That kind of makes love sound like the flu.

When Uncle Max spoke, he said something about how he never knew exactly how much laughter he was missing in his life until he met the manny. He didn't call him the manny. He called him Matthew. Uncle Max had a tear stream down his cheek like the little boy at the end of *Finding Neverland*.

The manny didn't say anything. He just gave Uncle Max a hug and asked Lulu to step forward to read her passage. I guess that's why Lulu knew about this surprise. She must have reached the age when parents don't keep secrets from their kids. I can't wait to reach that age. Mom will probably talk to me about diets, and Dad will talk about Old Spice and towel snapping. Locker-room talk.

Lulu stepped forward and opened up her copy of *To Kill a Mockingbird*. She cleared her throat, "Ahem," like she wanted everybody in the botanical garden and in the lobby to give her their attention. She spoke clearly and loudly, just like she had been taught in debate class.

"'I wanted you to see what real courage is, instead of getting the idea that courage is a man with a gun in his hand. It's when you know you're licked before you begin but you begin anyway and you see it through no matter what. You rarely win . . .'" Then Lulu paused before she looked up from her book and at Uncle Max and the manny and finished, "'But you sometimes do.'"

Lulu put her book down at her side, and the Elton John look-alike nodded at Uncle Max and the manny.

Uncle Max and the manny kissed. A few ladies who were walking by clapped. Lulu bowed and said, "Thank you very much," like they were clapping for her and not for Uncle Max and the manny. Then she joined in on Uncle Max and the manny's hug. She didn't even squeal because they were kissing.

I joined in too.

The tiny woman with the CD player pushed play. It was the same song that the manny had been singing along to at the concert. The one where butterflies are free to fly.

"'Someone saved my life tonight sugar bear.'"

Sugar Bear.

Dear Sarah,

We just ate dinner at a place called Circo to celebrate Uncle Max and the manny's wedding ceremony. It was so good and we felt like movie stars because the waiter came up at the end of the meal and told us that the meal had already been paid for and then he read a note that said, "Matty and Max, we're sorry we couldn't be there. We're so happy for you. Love, Mom and Dad and Captain Fantastic."

I can't wait to see you again,

Keats

P. S. Most people are really nice when you finally see them.